A RUDE AWAKENING FOR THE AMBITIOUS EX-BOYFRIEND

TEXAS REDEMPTION - BOOK 5

APRIL MURDOCK

This is a work of fiction. Any references to names, characters, organizations, places, events, or incidents are either products of the author's imagination or are used fictitiously.

CHECK OUT THIS FREE COWBOY ROMANCE!

If you enjoyed this sweet cowboy romance, you'll want to read *Finding Her Cowboy*! This story is where two best selling series meet with another heartwarming love story!

This stand alone story is an enemies to lovers whirlwind romance set in small town Texas where Thatcher Ranch and Bolton Ranch meet.

The Brothers of Thatcher Ranch series and the Billionaire Ranchers series comes together with cameo appearances by characters in each one.

Get a taste of each sweet romance series when city girl Adelaide and cowboy Maddox fall in love in the rancher's world Addy shouldn't fit into, but does.

Tap here to get your copy of Finding Her Cowboy

A RUDE AWAKENING FOR THE AMBITIOUS EX-BOYFRIEND

TEXAS REDEMPTION - BOOK 5

APRIL MURDOCK

Everything's bigger in Texas. Even redemption.

CHAPTER ONE

DR. AMBER CRAWFORD SMILED AS SHE LEFT LA MESA Medical Center with a spring in her step. It'd been a long yet productive shift today in the maternity ward. Eight separate expectant mothers with one routine delivery and no—thank heavens—surgeries required. Life was good. Maybe it was all that youthful energy. Being surrounded day in and day out by infants had this way of rejuvenating people, and she was no exception. The looks of awe on the faces of new parents never failed to warm her heart.

Of course, the single delivery she'd had required her to stay over, so now she was leaving three hours overdue. The upshot of this meant that she got to see the stunning desert sunset. El Paso, Texas, was often graced with spectacular skies, especially around this time of year. The heat that always sizzled the rugged landscape sometimes meant storms, but more often it meant sights like the fuchsia and lavender kaleidoscope above her. She loved June.

Though, to be fair, maybe she loved June simply because that meant time had moved her past May.

May tended not to be her most pleasant month. For some crazy reason, every major negative event in her life had happened during those thirty-one days. The time she'd been rear-ended and her car totaled after only having her license for a week? May. The only time she'd ever been dumped by a boyfriend? May. The first time as an obstetrician she'd ever had a baby be stillborn? May. Not to mention the fact that her birthday was May 17th. While most people celebrated their birthdays, Amber never had.

Since her mother had died trying to deliver her, the day had perpetually been more of a sad anniversary instead of a reason for balloons and cake.

So now that June had arrived, she felt better, even if her more rational, analytical side told her this sort of thing bordered on superstition. Regardless, she felt glad that May was over.

She stopped by Whole Foods to restock her depleting groceries. Amber hummed the song that had been playing over the PA system, something by Katy Perry she didn't know the words to, as she left the store. She'd just loaded her bags into the back of her Audi SUV when she caught movement out of the corner of her eye. Coming down Pitt Street was a large group of about two hundred people in running outfits, and she remembered. The local Oryx Challenge 5K Fun Run was today.

Amber paused for a brief moment as the joggers raced by, her hatchback still in the air. She'd been about to close it and hop in her vehicle when something blue stole her attention. It was one of the joggers, and he'd worn an eye-popping aqua tee and shorts; even his shoes matched. Since she always parked near the back of the parking lot so she'd get an extra bit of exercise, she stood no more than twenty feet from the marathoners. It was this closeness that proved to be her downfall because all at once she recognized the guy.

Snow cones! It was Troy Sykes, her ex.

Unfortunately, he was just as handsome as ever with his light blond hair, chiseled features, and athletic physique. In the nine years since she'd last seen him, he'd only become better looking. The guy could've easily graced the front of GQ or Men's Health, which was too bad since he'd nearly destroyed her. They'd gone to high school together where he helped his baseball team rank number one in their league. He'd been the most popular boy in the school as well as a grade older than she, and he'd acted as if she were invisible.

But later, when they'd both attended the University of Texas at El Paso, or UTEP for short, they'd both taken the same world history class. He'd asked to borrow her notes, which she'd readily supplied, and after that, he'd asked her out. Not believing her good luck, she'd given him a resounding yes. They'd dated from September to—yep, *May*—when he'd graduated. She'd attended the ceremony even though he hadn't specifically invited her.

Talk about a red flag. When the dude you're dating doesn't ask you to attend a major event of his, it's not exactly a good sign.

She shook her head at the memory. How guileless and blind could a girl be? When she'd caught up with him outside on the stadium's field, he'd been with his mom and little sister. Amber had waited for him to hold her hand or sling an arm around her shoulder, but he didn't. He'd seemed hesitant, so she took a step back.

"Amber," he'd said. "Didn't know you were going to be here."

The use of her name had been another warning beacon. On their first date, he'd told her she reminded him of a wood sprite from some fantasy movie and had nicknamed her "Sprite" from that second on. If he didn't call her Sprite, then he typically just shortened her name to Am. The fact that he'd done neither right then should've tipped her off to what was coming.

It didn't.

"Why wouldn't I be here? My boyfriend is graduating with his degree." Nerves had made her refer to him in the third person.

He'd looked at his family. "I'll be right back." Then, he'd turned to her. "Can I talk to you for a sec?"

Only then had she felt this cold sense of dread in the pit of her stomach, but she'd answered, "Sure."

"Listen, Am, I'm moving to Cali ahead of schedule."

"Ahead of schedule?" she'd parroted back to him like one of those dolls that repeat everything you say.

"Yeah, so I think it's better to just end things here. That way, I can get on with my life out there at UCLA."

She'd been so taken aback by this that she'd made him clarify. "By end things, do you mean break up with me?"

"Exactly," he'd said, looking as relieved as if he'd aced a difficult exam.

Amber had known he would attend UCLA Law School. What she hadn't known was that he'd planned to do it without even attempting to maintain their relationship. She'd thought they'd have the summer together before starting a long-distance thing, but apparently not.

"I'd so glad we can agree on this," he'd told her next, his expression cheerful. *Cheerful.* As if she hadn't been dying inside. "You're such a great girl. We've had a lot of good times together. Take care, all right?"

He hadn't even waited for a response before he'd traipsed back to his family, all smiles and ready to celebrate. That had been the last time she'd seen him until now.

Which meant it was time to get out of there. She had no desire to ever interact with the college boy who'd so cavalierly broken her heart, so she closed her hatchback and pivoted, aiming for her driver's side door.

"Sprite?" she heard a voice calling out to her. His, of course. "That really you?"

She felt severely tempted not to turn around, but she was a Southern girl who'd had politeness drilled into ever since she could remember. So, for cordiality's sake, she did. Troy was jogging in place on the road, a huge grin on his lips as he waved to her, a paragon of male beauty. Too bad he'd always known that about himself. To refer to him as conceited wouldn't do him justice.

No one could ever be as enamored with Troy as Troy was.

"It is you! I knew it. You look amazing. What have you been up to lately?" he asked, as if they'd parted on the best of terms. As if she hadn't fallen asleep crying over him every single night for a month.

"I'm a physician, an obstetrician," she said, then felt her face flame. She felt like she was flaunting her OB/GYN status, which was something she never did. But a teensy weensy and admittedly petty piece of her wanted him to know how well she'd done without him.

"Defense attorney," he pointed to his own chest as if they were in some weird, "Me Tarzan, you Jane" reenactment.

"Congratulations," she told him, then mentally kicked herself. Congratulations? She felt like the naïve twenty-year-old she'd been while with him. She twisted the small diamond eyebrow piercing she'd gifted herself for graduating as the valedictorian of her pre-med class. It gave her strength.

"Yeah, thanks," he said, not returning the sentiment. "You have your own practice, or are you at the hospital?"

"I'm at La Mesa."

"Cool. Catch ya later."

And he sprinted off as if they were dear old friends rather than the boyfriend who had thrown away his girlfriend with as much regard as he might throw away a gum wrapper.

In a daze, Amber sat behind her steering wheel, feeling as if she'd been hit by a Mack truck. She knew she should've responded differently to him somehow. Maybe stood up for herself or called him on what he'd done. She went through her evening activities with her brain fogged by woulda, coulda, shouldas. Would she feel better if she'd yelled at him and called him every name in the book? Should she have pretended that she couldn't hear him and peeled out of there like a NASCAR driver?

Thing was, that didn't match her style. Not only was she a Texas girl born and bred, she liked to consider herself a class act as well as independent. She did what she believed was the right thing as often as possible. She'd gone to med school for the sake of helping people, doing her best to keep other children from losing their mothers like she'd lost hers.

So, once again, she needed to rise above. She needed to not think of Troy Sykes anymore, so she wouldn't.

Amber believed she was doing great with her whole "I am woman, hear me roar, forget you, Troy Sykes!" initiative until halfway through dinner with her dad the next evening. He'd been talking about the seven-pound bass he'd caught over the weekend, but she'd lost the thread of their conversation for some reason.

"Earth to Amber... Hello..."

She tuned in just as her father flitted a hand in front of her face.

"Huh?"

"You okay, precious? You've been a bit out of it ever since you got here."

Well, *snow cones.*

"Sorry, Daddy, what were you saying? You caught a big fish, right?"

"Right," he said, chuckling at her.

Amber peeked up at him. She had so many of her dad's features. His eyes, nose, hair, everything. He used to call her his girly mini-me. The only things she'd gotten from her beautiful half-Korean mother were her slightly darker skin tone and her height. Or lack thereof. She was only 4'11", which meant she was typically the shortest adult in any room.

Prior to dying when Amber was a teenager, her grandma always corrected "short" to "petite," but they were one and the same. Either way, she couldn't reach half to three-quarters of the stuff in her kitchen without a step stool. At least she could adjust her patients' beds whenever necessary.

She wished Keiko Inthavong Crawford had lived for so many reasons. To talk to her and get to know her. To have mother-daughter lunches. To have had her assistance as she'd grown from a girl into a woman. To share with her mom what it was like to be physician. And, last but not least, to commiserate together over being vertically challenged.

"How many boys and girls yesterday?" he asked next, and she inwardly sighed at her and her dad's game. This question was his way of checking up on her. Any time one of her patients lost a baby—which was thankfully extremely rare—it devastated Amber. She tried to steel herself against it, and of course did everything in her power to save each and every child, but sometimes stillbirths and complications happened anyway.

"One baby boy. Lester," she answered.

"Lester?" her dad sounded appalled. "For a baby?"

"I know. Apparently, they were naming him for his great-uncle."

"That's just mean."

"Well, they did say they'd call him Les. That's not quite as bad."

Her dad was named Jeff, not Jeffrey, and with no middle name, so he had definite opinions on what to call an infant.

"So, you had a good day?" he asked, another form of fishing.

"Yep. Though it turned into a twelve-hour shift."

"Better than your residency days, though."

"Truth," she said, patting his forearm.

She'd been so exhausted during that time that she slept there in the on-call room at the hospital just for the extra few minutes of downtime. More than once her dad had shown up with sandwiches and orange juice, concerned that she wasn't getting enough to eat. Of course, she'd done the same for him whenever he worked long hours at the fire station, especially once he'd been promoted to captain. They were used to taking care of one another. That was the deal when it was Daddy and Daughter against the world.

Maybe having those days go through her mind put a warm enough expression on her face that her dad quit digging, because the remainder of their dinner went back to normal. She didn't know why Troy's appearance should bother her anyway. It wasn't like he'd come back into her life in any significant manner.

She hugged her dad before she left, feeling lighter just by spending time with him. It would be silly to let things slip out of perspective. Stiffening her spine, she drove home, purposely focused on anything but Troy Sykes.

CHAPTER TWO

"WHO WAS THAT?" BRETT GUERRERO, TROY'S BEST BUDDY, asked him.

"Back in college, she was my girl."

"Yeah?" Brett sounded surprised, and Troy couldn't blame him.

In Cali, Troy had kept everything casual with the women he hung out with, not once engaging in any sort of serious relationship. He hadn't had time for it. But now that Brett was hooking him up with this sweet position at the firm where his best bro had just made partner—a place Troy felt sure he could make partner in a couple of months himself —his schedule should open up enough for more of a personal life again.

How lucky was it that he happened to bump into Amber again? He'd thought about her many times over the years. Her tiny stature. Her pixie-like hair and features. She was adorable. That was why his nickname for her was so fitting. And it felt almost like fate was throwing her into his path. How awesome was that?

But then, Troy had fantastic luck. He always had. From elementary school on, everyone had loved him: teachers, principals, coaches, other students. He'd been popular, had kept straight A's on his report card, and had thrown constant strikes with his pitching arm. A smart jock who'd been good-looking to boot.

What wasn't to like?

Nothing. Even if he did say so himself.

He was a winner, and everyone loved a winner. He had a photographic memory which allowed him to catalog and hold it in his brain for future use. It made everything quite convenient.

Troy had been utilizing it on the regular to defend his long roster of clients. He'd left behind that roster now, but he wasn't worried in the least. He knew scrounging up some new ones would be like shooting fish in a barrel. People got arrested and needed defending in each state, and Texas had some of the strictest laws in the nation. He'd find plenty of clients and defend them just like he had been doing for the past five years. It'd be fun.

Amber Crawford, though. He let her name wind paths through his memory as he and Brett maintained their steady pace through the final leg of the marathon. He couldn't believe how different yet the same she looked. With the blonde streaks shooting through her short yet curly chestnut hair, as well as the piercing glittering from one eyebrow, she seemed like someone a bit edgier than the meek and mild girl he'd once dated.

Of course, she'd always been beautiful. Troy didn't hang with any chick that wasn't gorgeous, especially not long term. But the years had been uber kind to her. If anything, she was even prettier now than she'd been before. And that was saying something.

Part of the reason he'd gotten such a thrill out of being with her was because of how cute and dainty she was. She was an itty-bitty thing—she barely came up to his chest—and he liked towering over her. The fact that she laughed easily at his jokes was a big bonus too. He'd enjoyed the whole hero worship thing she'd had going on for him; it'd been an awesome ego boost.

After he threw on a burst of speed so he could beat Brett's time, because of course he needed to beat his friend, he tossed around the idea of hitting Amber back up for a date. Now that he was back home in El Paso after crushing it over in LA, having her as his arm candy at corporate parties and other professional get-togethers appealed to him. She'd adored him, so he was certain she'd be amenable to his plan.

So once he'd showered and dressed, he put a reminder in his phone to contact her the next day. Which he did. Bright and early. As he dialed her old cell number, he wondered if he'd get through. Had she changed it?

"You have reached Dr. Amber Crawford. If you're in labor and your contractions are less than five minutes apart, have someone go ahead and drive you to the hospital. Do not drive yourself. If you feel like something is wrong, don't hesitate to call 911." Beep.

He decided to forego leaving his own message behind since he wanted to speak to her directly, so he disconnected and dialed her again. When she didn't pick up, he kept dialing. He wouldn't give up, no matter how many times he had to call her. This was a method that he often employed in his professional dealings that worked. One thing he knew for sure—persistence paid off.

Finally, on the fifth ring, she accepted his call. *Yes*!

"Hello," she sounded harried, so he smiled, knowing she could hear the smile in his voice. It was an old trick he'd learned back in law school, a persuasive technique.

"Hey there, Sprite. It was so nice seeing you again yesterday."

"Troy, I really don't appreciate you calling me 'Sprite' after nine years. Especially at the crack of dawn and considering everything that happened between us. Also, I find that name unflattering."

Whoa. Was she still mad over their split? He never realized she was one to hold a grudge.

"Oh, come on. Don't be upset. That's all water under the bridge."

She released a sharp huff. "Maybe it's water under the bridge for you, but for me…" she trailed off, so he chimed back in.

"That was a long time ago. Can't we just let bygones be bygones?"

"My boyfriend broke up with me at his graduation ceremony surrounded by his classmates, family, and friends."

"Yeah," he agreed. That's what he remembered as well.

"Then, that same boyfriend acted as if, after nine months together, he wanted to get rid of me."

In truth, he had. He'd been too young to settle down. Not that he wanted to settle down now, either, but having a fresh young thing on his arm every night meant a lot of picking and choosing. He'd rather streamline the process and go back to having a girlfriend. Having the same woman consistently around would simplify his life. And Amber had filled the role before. Why was she fighting him on this? Most women were happy to fall at his feet.

"We had a good time, though, didn't we?"

"That's not the point." She sounded seriously angry, angrier than she had a moment ago. "Why would I ever agree to go out with you again after you burned me so badly?"

Oh, she wanted him to apologize, that was what this was. Good thing he was an expert at feigning them. It was a mere matter of agreeing with the injured party. "You're right. I shouldn't have ended things like I did." Followed by the sincere-sounding amends making. "And I'm sorry. You're a great girl who I enjoyed being with. I should've made that clearer at the time. If you give me another chance, I will." He'd take her out and spoil her, get her back on his side.

There was a pause on the line, and he silently pumped his fist in victory. He had her!

"Be that as it may, I'm not interested in seeing you again, Troy. I have somewhere to be."

And then, she disconnected. She'd concluded their call without agreeing to go out with him again. Which was so not cool.

For a few heartbeats, he felt put off by this setback. He didn't like hearing no or failing in any way. The only time he'd ever faced such a thing was with the man who'd fathered him. Not that Brooks Sykes had done much fathering when it came to him or his baby sister, Mia. When he'd been little, Troy had watched Brooks float in and out of their lives as he pleased. Then, when Troy had been five, shortly after Mia's birth, Brooks had floated out permanently.

Years later, Troy discovered that Brooks had chosen to leave his original family for another woman. That while he and Mia had been at home with their mom, their so-called dad had been off gallivanting with someone else.

If he could go back in time and express himself to the man, he'd say, "Good riddance. Don't let the door hit you on the way out." Or maybe something ruder and cruder.

A wave of depression washed over him then, but he shook it off. No use spending energy worrying about the waste of space who'd sired him. Particularly when he had other more positive prospects to think about. Coming back home. His new job, which he knew would be epic. And his pursuit of Amber. If he framed his situation with her as a challenge, that altered everything. She may not have said yes *yet*, but she would. He'd make certain of it.

Buoyed by this refreshing outlook, he rubbed his hands together, peering out at the sunken pool that was only feet away from his back door. The water shone in the color of pure turquoise beneath the hot Texas sun; this pool was larger than the one he'd had in LA, and it even had a waterfall. He loved listening to the sound of the miniature falls rushing in from the opposite side of his diving board. He'd never regret buying a property that fit with his billionaire lifestyle.

His new place was a two-story, four-bed, four-bath with eleven thousand square feet. Out its windows the Franklin Mountains—better known to previous generations as the Las Sierras de los Mansos—stood sentry over El Paso, their craggy brown peaks visible from nearly every room. It had a huge, covered patio, a stained-glass front entryway, a gazebo at the other end of the pool, and a chef's kitchen. Not that he could cook. He was relatively helpless in the kitchen, but having all this was about status. When he invited Brett and Mia over with the rest of the partners, he wanted to show them that he was one of them.

Because he was.

He also needed to show Amber at some point. If she witnessed the luxury of his not-at-all-humble abode, maybe it would help to win her over.

Troy thought back to the time when they'd been together. She'd liked to laugh and had a somewhat nerdy sense of humor. He could totally work with that. He pulled up some jokes on his phone. At first, he found knock-knock jokes, but those were more for kids, right? He next found some he found funny, but they'd probably be too racy for a good girl like her.

Then, he remembered that she'd had an affinity for the Far Side comics by Gary Larson. She'd even had a day-by-day calendar of them in her dorm room, not that she'd ever allowed him inside. But he often stood outside her room to pick her up for dates, and she'd post the comics she liked best up on the corkboard attached to her door. More than once he'd laughed out loud at these, garnering the attention of the other female residents nearby.

He always felt amused by how annoyed they'd look when they'd step into their hallway, bathrobes flying around them, only to demur the second they caught sight of him. Well, a couple of the girls had screamed and slammed their doors on him, but most had demurred. Of course, Amber would appear, and he'd yank his focus back to her. Usually. He liked to flirt—sometimes right in front of her —though he'd never gone after anybody else while he'd been with Amber. College had been a good time, but cheating had been his father's game. It'd never be his.

Man, why did Brooks keep popping into his head? It was as irritating as a rock in his shoe.

Shaking the memory of the man off for the second time that day, he spent a few minutes searching the web, chuckling at the individual comics he found hilarious and saving them in his phone for future use.

All he needed to do now was wear Amber down.

CHAPTER THREE

AMBER KEPT HER HEAD UP AND HER FACE CAREFULLY BLANK until she reached the single restroom down the hall. Once inside with the door locked, she dropped the façade and rested the back of her head against the door, blowing out such a forceful breath that it made her bangs fly away from her forehead. It'd been a long day. Five deliveries at the hospital. Then, she'd gone to volunteer at the free women's health clinic downtown and experienced a close call.

It'd been so close, in fact, that she'd had to put all her skills into saving both mother and child. The baby had been breech, which was never optimal, but then the mom had gotten tired—totally understandable—and with tears flooding down her face, she'd told Amber she couldn't push anymore.

"It's either you push now, or we call an ambulance to take you to the hospital and prep you for surgery, Kristen. I know you can do this. You're strong enough to keep going."

And fortunately, with that, Kristen had reached deep down and given it her all. The baby's cry could be heard a moment later, and Amber had almost cried herself in relief. Poor Kristen had been in labor for over twenty-four hours, the final ten at the clinic.

It was one of those things most people didn't realize unless they'd been through the birthing process. Not only was labor hard on a woman's system due to the pain involved, it could also do a number on the mother's psyche. Many people could bear up under a difficult situation for a while, but if it went on too long, they began to think it would never end.

They'd start to doubt their abilities and their own strength. And yet, time and again, Amber had witnessed women do the almost impossible simply by being bound and determined to follow through and bring their child into the world. Encouragement could often be the key. The body was a miracle, and a body's systems working in concert to give birth, even more so. Not to mention the bouncing baby blessing at the end.

It was why Amber loved what she did so much.

But sometimes, even she needed a minute to collect herself.

Two hours ago, Kristen's child had been in real distress. If the woman hadn't rallied like she had, Amber would've been forced to do a caesarean right there at the clinic, and with that came an even higher chance of complications. Surgery might be mandatory to save lives, but it could take them as well. Amber knew that things could go wrong, and if everything went wrong all at once, lives could be lost.

Like her own mother's had.

Thankfully, it hadn't come to that this time. Not that Amber minded the surgery aspect itself. She went out of her way to stay abreast of all the most recent updates and surgical breakthroughs. At least once a month, she attended seminars or continuing education classes to keep her skills as sharp as humanly possible. She did everything she could to provide her patients with the best care even if it meant she lost sleep and any chance for a personal life.

It was worth it.

Though at times, like today, she wondered if she might look back at the end of her life and regret her own lack of a husband and children. Currently, she had no room for either. Her colleague and best friend, Grace Pendergrass, had mentioned opening up their own practice together, but so far, Amber had put such a notion off. They'd need to find or construct the appropriate building, purchase the correct and most up-to-date equipment, and hire a staff, including at least a couple of nurse practitioners capable of filling in when either of the two main obstetricians were out.

Grace's dream was to have more control of their own shifts and how they ran things. Much of that came from her best friend being a wife and mother looking to optimize her time at home. It sounded great to Amber in principle, but the upfront work required seemed like too much of a hassle. Not to mention that neither of them had been able to carve out the hours necessary to even begin to put any of those millions of pieces into place; her bestie volunteered there at the clinic just like she did. So, she doubted their practice would come to fruition anytime soon.

Nice as it would be.

After coming out of the bathroom, she heard her cell chime in her desk drawer. Usually, she didn't bother to check it during work hours. Yet, since she had a free minute, she glanced at the screen.

Troy Sykes. Ugh.

Troy: Something to giggle at.

He'd sent her an attachment of some kind. She was afraid to look. When they'd been college kids, their senses of humor had been similar most of the time, and she doubted that he'd matured at all since then. She didn't want to see what he'd sent, so she wouldn't. She took a bite of her peanut-butter-filled celery, along with a swig of her purified water. Hmmm. What had he sent her? And why? The thought was burning a hole of curiosity through her.

He wouldn't have sent her something tacky, right? Something inappropriate? She couldn't be sure of that. *Something to giggle at*. Obviously, he found whatever he'd sent funny. Would she? Oh, for the love of…

She clicked on the text, opening it up to see a Far Side cartoon strip.

The first picture depicted a shark out in the ocean calling to the people on the beach, "Bear! Bear!" and of course, the sunbathers were hurtling into the water towards said shark. She shook her head at it. So goofy. But that wasn't the only image. She scrolled down to spot another one that had no words but showed a man sitting on his porch. He had a wooden leg which a cat was actively utilizing as a scratching post.

She felt her mouth lift into a grin. Okay, that was pretty funny. But then she noticed one more. This picture had aliens on a flying saucer surrounded by human onlookers. There were stairs exiting the saucer with three aliens at the top, but at the bottom, one of the aliens had clearly tripped and fallen, its eyestalks looking crossed. The caption said, "Wonderful! Just wonderful… So much for instilling them with a sense of awe."

For whatever reason, that struck her as hilarious, and she released a snort, then a snicker. Still, she didn't want to be entertained by Troy Sykes, the most uncaring boyfriend-abruptly-turned-ex in the universe. The only problem was every time she remembered that silly comic with the aliens, she had to bite back a smile.

And over the next few days, the Far Side texts continued. Some were lowbrow, while some were more cerebral, but at least half of them hit their mark. There was the one where the lady's husband was trapped in the couch and she only cared that she'd found her hairbrush underneath the cushions. There was the one where God was creating the herbivores of the animal kingdom and remarked, "Hmmmm, I'd better make some things that eat you guys."

Grace had overheard her that time, and Amber had to tell her what was going on. She'd already told her bestie all about how she'd bumped into Troy and how he'd broken up with her once upon a time.

"He's attempting to get on my good side by sending me cartoons," Amber explained.

Blowing a harsh gust of air out of her mouth, Grace scoffed, "Like that'll work. You could block him, you know."

"I know."

Maybe she should block him. She'd considered the notion more than once but still hadn't done it.

After they each did a little more reading about the newest research into nutrition for high-risk pregnancies in those over forty, Grace spoke up again.

"So, what did he send?"

Amber reached for her phone again to show her. "They're ridiculous, aren't they?"

"No, they're funny. He, on the other hand, is crazy if he thinks a few pics he lazily pulled up from online are going to be enough to make you forgive him."

Amber high-fived her. "Exactly."

The thing was, that wasn't all he did. Over the next few weeks, he not only sent her comics, he also sent her huge bouquets of flowers—lilacs, her favorite—as well as chocolate-covered cherries (another favorite.) She'd been shocked that he even remembered what she liked since they hadn't been a couple for so many years. Yet, he did. She'd known he had an eidetic memory for recalling words he'd read, but maybe it worked for the past likes of old girlfriends as well.

It wasn't enough, though. Not by a long shot. Which made her worry when she found herself softening toward him. What he'd done to her was *not* nice, she knew this, yet she'd begun to look forward to his goofy texts.

He'd call and leave voicemails about some of the great times they'd had back in the day. Nearly all of his shenanigans had been over the top, but for the first time in years, she started to remember them with fondness instead of fury. After a full nonstop barrage of this nonsense, he arrived at the hospital close to the end of her shift. He wore a fancy suit and tie, carried another even bigger bouquet of lilacs, as well as a larger box of chocolates. As she came out to the waiting area, he made a spectacle of himself by dropping down on both knees.

"Am, beautiful girl, go out with me again."

With the exception of Grace, several of the family and friends of the patients and many of the staff members got dopey and romantic expressions on their faces. He was making a gesture, a grand one, and everyone looked at her to see if she'd accept it.

It was easy to get caught up in all of it, especially when he got several of them to chant with him, "Say yes. You know you want to."

No wonder the guy was a lawyer.

Embarrassed now, she ducked her head and whispered in his ear, "Please stop."

"Is that a yes?" he asked back, not bothering to keep his voice low.

"Troy... I..."

"Come on, now. I'll keep making you laugh. Every day. You know we can have a good time together."

She did, but she also knew he could yank the rug out from under her. Still, he wouldn't go to all this effort for nothing, right? He must really want to date her again. It wasn't like she had to marry him or even give him a piece of her heart. It was just a date or two, for heaven's sake. So she took a deep breath.

"All right. Yes."

CHAPTER FOUR

THE BEST THING ABOUT TAKING AMBER OUT AGAIN WAS HOW simple it all was. They didn't need any real time to get to know one another because they basically already did. So Troy felt perfectly comfortable slipping right back into the mode he'd been in the last time they'd shared company together. Back at UTEP, he'd been a baseball jock at the top of his game who'd been lavished with all the positive attention he could want.

Now was even better since he was on the cusp of greatness at the law firm of Bertram, Rockford, and Guerrero. The partners were already impressed with him, had offered him a hefty signing bonus, and over the past month, Brett had been priming him for the part. Troy could already see it. Soon, the sign outside of their building would say Bertram, Rockford, Guerrero, and *Sykes*. It was inevitable at this point.

Life was good.

Having Amber by his side turned out to be his icing on the cake. He'd invited her to one social gathering so far, and she was so much less shy and awkward than she'd been in college that she slid into place next to him like some sort of round peg. She came across as intelligent and articulate without showing him up.

It'd been like a dream.

And just this morning, Brett had popped into his office to offer him the case of a lifetime. The defendant was a general contractor of several housing developments on both the western and eastern sides of El Paso. He was known for his TV commercials, radio spots, and internet ads featuring his onetime winner of the Miss Texas pageant wife and three daughters under the age of five.

Troy read over the brief. It looked like the homeowners were going after this Paul Adams dude because of subpar building practices, but the local inspector had already provided an affidavit saying all his company's builds were within code. The case was drawing a lot of attention through the local media outlets due to the guy's high profile in the area.

There were some pieces of evidence that went against his client. Photographs of unfinished work and a mistake where someone had put a door in a place that wasn't in the original blueprints. But his client had asked for some extra time to correct those issues and had been refused.

To Troy, the case against Paul Adams, though present, should be weak enough to cast that shadow of doubt on. And using his skills, he could definitely poke holes in the proof the prosecuting attorney had provided. It felt so amazing to know that the firm trusted him with this. Once he won, Troy would step up in the ranks and gracefully accept the promotion they'd offer him.

He heard the special tone he'd assigned Amber's text messages, the chorus of *Here I Go Again* by Whitesnake, a classic eighties rock band. Hearing it made him smirk. At the beginning, Am hadn't reached out to him much, instead leaving the pursuing and wooing to him. So, he'd continued. But here she was, reaching out to him.

He glanced down at his screen.

Sprite: Pizza and the Rangers sound good. What time tomorrow?

He liked having her listed under her nickname even if she didn't care for it. He'd just have to keep her away from the contacts inside his phone.

Troy: Whenever you can get over to my place. Game starts at seven.

Sprite: Unless I have a delivery that goes over, I'll be there.

Troy: You're the best.

That was his trademark send-off. He'd used it ever since law school. Every girl he'd dated was told that she was "the best." It sounded caring without actually requiring him to show any specific feelings for them. It didn't invite any "I love yous," but was still a compliment. And since he hadn't used that casual refrain with Amber the first time, she didn't even know what he was doing. He enjoyed staying one step ahead at all times. It was what made him such an excellent attorney.

Besides, with Amber, things were convenient. Most of the time she didn't expect anything out of him other than a few minutes of his time on the phone every evening. It was such a workable setup for him. And their actual dates had become so laidback. Because she grew up with a single dad, she liked sports and was satisfied to hang out at his place with a casual dinner in front of his big screen TV. She never overstayed her welcome either.

It was awesome.

His phone rang again, but this time it wasn't Amber, it was his mother. He felt a niggle of impatience but instantly buried it. He and his mom were tight. And now that his baby sister Mia had married his best friend, she no longer lived there at home. His mom was all alone, which meant he couldn't ignore her, even when busy.

"Hey, Ma."

"Hi there, baby. How's my handsome boy?"

"Staying handsome," he quipped. It was kind of their thing.

"Did I interrupt you, Troy? Are you busy?"

"That's okay. You doing all right over there?"

His mother lived only about ten blocks away. He'd moved her there as soon as he started making money in LA. Not that she was as broke as she'd been when Brooks had left. For a couple of years, his family had been on public assistance, but then, his mom had started to write this series of historical fiction. It took her a few books to get going, but then they sold well, even if she'd never become a millionaire or anything. She still wrote them to this day.

"I'm fine. Don't you worry about me. I'm just glad you're back home."

She and Mia were Troy's most pertinent reasons for coming back, though he trusted Brett with his sister. She was so happy now. But his mom remained alone. She'd always taken care of him and Mia, so returning the favor and making her proud was one of his top priorities.

"Brett made sure I caught this incredible case. It's high profile with high dollar amounts and goes to court next week. Can't wait to drag the prosecution through the dirt."

His mother laughed. She'd always loved to hear him smack talk.

"Mia tells me you're seeing some girl. That she's your girlfriend."

Dang it, he hadn't wanted to discuss Amber with his mom yet. He'd kept his relationship with her back in college secret from his family because all their time together had been on campus. So no one knew his history with Amber but Brett, whom he might just have to murder if he let any more cats out of the bag where Mia was concerned.

"It's new." Was all he'd say.

"Are you not going public yet?"

"We're public," Troy hedged. "We're just busy. She's a doctor over at Le Mesa Medical Center. So far we haven't even had much time for ourselves, so…"

"Yet she's your girlfriend?" his mom challenged.

"We're exclusive."

Technically, that in and of itself made Amber his girlfriend in his eyes, even if she hadn't said yes to that yet. He asked her more than once and knew she'd say yes eventually. Nevertheless, he hadn't been ready to address this with his mother. He liked to keep his life compartmentalized, always had.

"Well, if you're still with her by the time Mia's birthday rolls around in August, I want you to bring her over. Introduce her to us properly."

Mia's birthday was still six weeks away. That should give him enough time to prepare.

"Will do, Ma, but I gotta go."

"Love you, baby."

"You, too."

"Sorry, I'm late," Amber rushed in, but she'd changed out of her scrubs, which Troy felt thankful for. Her scrubs were so baggy and unflattering on her. Not that he didn't know better than to tell her so. The jeans and pink tee she wore looked way better. "What inning are we in?"

"The fourth," he answered as she sat next to him on his huge leather sectional. He didn't bother getting her a plate or anything. He'd shown her where everything was. Once she was seated, he asked, "Hey, can you hand me the marinara for these breadsticks?" He'd forgotten to grab the small, closed container in the kitchen. She remained still for a beat, but his concentration had gone back to the baseball game. "Am?"

"I've just spent ten hours on my feet, and you want me to wait on you hand and foot?" she asked, her tone cool.

The action on his television screen paused for a commercial, so he stood. Without looking at her, he went to his kitchen, grumbling under his breath, "Don't know what the big deal is. All I asked for was one tiny cup of sauce." He'd thought he'd kept his complaints inaudible, but apparently not.

"I only caught part of that, but I really don't appreciate you grumbling about me," she informed him, in a bit of a snit.

Busted. But this was his home where he could say whatever he wanted.

"Yesterday was my volunteer day which amounts to a double shift," she went on, and he inwardly sighed. "Now, today, you're griping at me…"

"I'm not griping, though I don't know why you'd want to waste your time at that clinic anyway."

"Waste my time?" She gawked at him as if appalled, lines furrowing the flawless skin between her eyes. "Working at that clinic means I'm saving lives who would likely be lost otherwise. Not everyone has the money or resources that we have, Troy. Just because they're poor doesn't mean they don't deserve to be taken care of too."

Troy didn't know why people stayed poor. His mom hadn't, even with two kids to raise on her own. Besides, there were scholarships and grants and things. Why didn't they just go to school so they could start a good career like he had? Still, as he glanced over at Amber, he knew that would be the wrong thing to say.

"You're right." Those two words had saved him so much grief in his life. Arguments between himself and his mom or his sister always fizzled as soon as he said this, and the same was true of Amber. "I guess I'm just stressed because I have that important case starting up in court next week." He'd told her about it, so working it into the discussion now felt natural. Also, it served as a great excuse.

"I'm sorry if you're stressed, but I'm not that little doormat you dated years ago. Just so you know."

Yeah, he knew. This wasn't the first time she'd reminded him. He contemplated for a minute how he should respond. If she exasperated him enough, he'd break up with her, but other than these fleeting spats, they'd been getting along all right. And there was something cozy about having Amber in his home that he liked. He wasn't ready to give up her companionship. At least, not yet.

"You're right," he told her again on auto pilot, then went into his default fake apology mode. "Sorry. Want some parmesan?"

"Please."

And just like that, they were right back on track again.

CHAPTER FIVE

SOMETIMES AMBER FELT HER HACKLES RISE AROUND TROY. There'd be this underlying feeling of unease that made her wonder what on earth she was doing with this guy. But then he'd apologize and make things right between them for another day.

At work she felt like she had some of the sharpest instincts imaginable. Anytime she felt the least bit apprehensive about a delivery, she'd stay to complete it herself, and almost inevitably complications would arise.

Yet, when it came to romance, those instincts seemed to be missing. Her dates back in high school and college pre-Troy had been unmitigated disasters with those boys walking all over her. Then, Troy had done his thing.

Her track record didn't lend itself to her feeling confident.

Not that she didn't enjoy hanging out with him now. She and Troy had a lot in common at the end of the day. An interest in sports. A passion for their jobs. They both made a good living too, though she knew his bank account far outstripped hers. *Snow cones*, they even liked the exact same pizza toppings.

Yet she didn't feel certain about staying with him. Maybe it was because of the bad blood they had between them, but as often as she laughed at his Far Side texts and felt a thrill at receiving his flattery, she never quite felt like she could lower her guard in his presence.

Then she felt guilty. No man was perfect. And how much trouble had he gone to in order to prove himself worthy of her again? Her office had taken on the permanent scent of lilacs because he sent her so many so often. She wouldn't run out of chocolate candies anytime soon either. She should relax and be happy rather than sabotaging something that was mostly working.

The following Monday was slower than usual, and for the first time since they'd started going out again, Troy hadn't texted her his usual triad of cartoons. She peeked at yesterday's. The selection had included a skier heading towards a snowy mountain with a sign that said, "Danger: Avalanche Area," as two men meandered by playing a set of mobile bass drums and some enormous cymbals.

The second showed an anxiety-ridden feline in a submarine with the caption, "The living torment of Jacques Cousteau's cat." And the last had a rodent in a jail cell lamenting, "I would have gotten away scot-free if I had just gotten rid of the evidence, but what can I say? I'm a pack rat."

If she wasn't mistaken, the commencement of his big trial had started today, so he must be too entrenched in the courtroom to send her things. Bizarrely, she missed his silly messages. She also missed the way he'd kissed her back in college, which was ridiculous because she'd been the one to pull away every time he'd tried to lock his lips to hers this time around. Being with Troy felt like this constant tug-of-war. They laughed together, then they fought. She wanted his kiss but wouldn't let him actually do it.

He'd made another attempt after their pizza and baseball night last Friday. He'd been giving her this intense stare with his bright sky-blue eyes. The man had looked so attractive that evening, it'd been absurd. Blond hair kissed by sunlight and the lightest scruff of five o'clock shadow.

If she hadn't known he hailed from Texas, she would've believed him to be the surfer boy from California he resembled. An intelligent, educated, gorgeous guy who accepted it when she offered him a hug instead of the kiss he wanted. He always hugged her back too.

She really should be more grateful.

Grace came barreling out of an exam room, alarm blanching her face. "Amber, I need you to take the rest of my patients for the afternoon. This patient's blood pressure is off the charts. I'm going to need to do a caesarean right away."

"I've got you," Amber promised her. "Send a nurse out to me if you need anything."

Grace did send for her. The mother had a set of twins, both of whom flatlined at one point. It took Amber and Grace working together to resuscitate each infant and get them squared away in the NICU. It'd been a harrowing day that left her and her best friend emotionally exhausted. Due to this, the two women left as soon as they could, needing the reprieve. Luckily, neither of them would be on call or scheduled to volunteer that night.

Still, for the first time since she and Troy had started up together, she felt this compulsion to confide in him about her work woes. She wanted to lay her head on his wide shoulder and have him tell her everything would be okay.

So she waited until she knew the courts had adjourned and sent him a text.

Amber: I've had a rough day. Can you come over?

She'd never invited him over before, so this was a big step forward. Amber was putting herself out on a metaphorical limb by trusting him to be there for her and felt a surge of nervousness. It didn't help that ten minutes went by without a response from him. She debated on sending him a second text or calling him and settled on the direct dial, which went to voicemail.

"Troy, it's Amber." She exhaled noisily. "I've had a bad day and… I'd like for you to…" *Remind me that I love my job. Make me feel less alone. Loop your arms around me and hold me for a while. Be the boyfriend I need you to be.* "Well, I'd like for you to come over. But if you'd rather, I'll go over there instead. Let me know, okay?" Beep.

An hour passed. Troy must have been backed up with meetings or something because she'd heard nothing. She retrieved her bath salts, poured a healthy dollop of bubble bath into her claw-footed tub, and sank into the nearly scalding water. Amber left her phone in the bamboo caddy she kept attached to the side of the tub, just in case.

Why hadn't he called her back yet?

Amber had just stepped out and wrapped herself in a towel when her phone rang at long last.

"Troy," she said, relief in her voice. "I'm so glad you called."

"What do you need, Am?" he asked her tersely. Had he not read her text or listened to her voice message?

"Oh, are you still at work?"

"Just left."

"Okay. I had a bad day and would like to see you. I could…" She felt vulnerable all of a sudden, the back of her eyes stinging as if she were leaping off an emotional ledge. She almost changed her mind and decided to come up with some excuse, then at the last minute, pushed onward. "I could really use one of your hugs."

He let out a sigh. A loud one. "You know, now's not the best time."

Her hackles lifted again. He should *want* to be there for her. "But… Troy—"

"What part of no don't you understand?" he cut her off. "I've got too much going on right now. Too much to deal with whatever piddling problem you're whining about too."

She gasped at the harshness of his tone. He might as well have slapped her across the face. Amber considered herself an articulate woman, but this took her a beat to recover from. Once she did, she became the unflinching physician who'd grown accustomed to being screamed at in the delivery room.

"I'm going to assume you've had a bad day as well to lash out at me so viciously."

"It has been a bad day," he bit out, ignoring the rest of her comment. She awaited his apology, though this time wasn't certain she'd take it. "In fact, you know what? I think we need to call it quits."

She pressed her cell closer to her ear. Had she heard him correctly?

"Did you just say call it *quits*?" she asked, incredulously.

"Yeah. I don't have time for this right now." He sounded… nonchalant. Even flippant. "Maybe once this case is over, you can come back, but I don't know. I can't make any promises."

"You are *not* breaking up with me, Troy. Not again. I don't believe you," her voice left her as part hiss, part snarl. He couldn't do this, he wouldn't, not after jumping through so many hoops to reunite with her.

"I'm just too preoccupied. I'll hit you up afterwards, maybe." He used the term "maybe" with all the emotional depth of someone rescheduling a follow-up appointment, not ending a relationship. A relationship that had barely been glued back together.

Before she could make any further objections, she heard a click, then nothing at all. He'd disconnected, abandoning their conversation and leaving her to listen to the silence.

For the longest time, she stood there in her towel with her phone held up to her ear in one hand, stunned. Then, her knees losing their strength, she collapsed on the side of her tub. Her brain had turned into some amorphous blob, giving her nothing useful as feedback. That had not just happened. It couldn't have. Troy wouldn't pull a repeat after all this time. He couldn't possibly be that callous.

How could Troy Sykes go to college at the same school she had, go out with her his entire senior year, break up with her in a single sentence, return a full nine *years* later, beg her to go out with him for a second time, and convince her they should be a couple again, only to dump her over the phone a mere four weeks later?

What type of rational, upstanding human being did that to another?

Twice?

Worse still, was she the easiest mark on the planet or what? She blinked, upset, trying to remember that awful saying. *Fool me once, shame on you. Fool me twice, shame on me.* Shame on *her*. And Amber did feel ashamed. Ashamed and enraged and a hundred other emotions besides.

Needing an outlet for her ire, she stood, wound up like the pitcher Troy Sykes had once been, and threw her phone as hard as she could. It flew full force into her bathroom mirror. The glass shattered, leaving dangerous silver shards all over her floor tiles, a hazardous proposition for her bare feet. She saw that the screen of her cell had been damaged as well, a spiderweb of cracks spanning across its surface, and she didn't even care.

A rage unlike any she'd ever known incinerated her system, and though she'd never hated anyone before, now she had a real contender.

How dare that man traipse back into her life and pull a fast one *again*.

Seething, blood pressure skyrocketing to dangerous levels, she shoved her hands into her hair and glared at the devastation around her. Amber didn't know how long she stood there frozen in place as her breaths ever so gradually evened out, but at length, her anger ebbed into something closer to righteous indignation. Now that she was thinking more clearly, she lowered herself, balancing on the balls of her feet to start to clean up the devastation she'd created.

As she cleaned, not moving to keep from slicing her feet open, she noticed her phone lighting up with a reminder of some sort. She squinted over at it and noted the date and time. 9:07 PM. July 25th.

A bizarre calm settled over her then, and mindlessly, she dropped the shards in her hands into the bathroom waste basket. Taking a giant step back from the debris and destruction, she ended up in her hallway. Dropping to her backside as her shoulder pressed into the door of her linen closet, all the tension, horror, and fury melted as a single realization filtered through her mind.

This lousy, hurtful, *evil* thing had just happened to her, and it wasn't even May.

CHAPTER SIX

Troy pocketed his phone and continued crossing the parking lot to his Hummer. Yeah, he wished he didn't have to cut Amber loose, but he needed to laser focus on his trial. And that meant zero distractions. He felt the most fleeting twinge of regret over splitting with her, but then he thought about how his day had gone in court and pushed her from his mind. Today had been a train wreck, there was no other way of putting it. He had to figure out how to fix this proverbial mess before things became even worse.

Except for the constant shouted queries made by local reporters on their way inside the courthouse, the proceedings had started out normal enough. The prosecution had called their witnesses and presented their case against his client Paul Adams. On cross-examination, Troy had questioned every source of proof they'd had and pointed out that Mr. Adams had made good on his promise to remedy any problems. He also evoked sympathy for his client by showing that the man's mother had just died, a possible cause for his temporary lack of oversight.

Then, a sucker punch had hit Troy right in the gut. The prosecution had asked to be able to show some new evidence that had just come to light. Troy protested, of course, but the judge had dismissed his objections. This fresh information came in the form of another group of witnesses with much more incriminating photos. Three different houses had been built and furnished, only to have a segment of the roof fall after the homeowners had already moved in, causing extensive damage. While no one had been hurt, it was only chance that had made that so.

The prosecution ripped into his client, who was left to stammer and look guilty. Troy had tried his best to shore up Adams' good reputation, but unless he could assert that those pictures had been photoshopped, things were looking bad.

Over the ensuing week, the hits just kept on coming. The prosecution had not one but two whining homeowners up on the stand, saying that they'd used all their savings to purchase a home that was now unlivable. The jury watched with sympathetic expressions. He was losing them. Especially when the second homeowner had announced this little nugget.

"And Paul Adams' company still hasn't lifted a finger to repair our home to this day."

Was that true? Seriously?

In his head, Troy thought back to everything he'd read about this case. He could see every word of the original transcripts in his mind, but nothing there helped him. He cross-examined this second lady, plastering on his "sad" face and then attempting to discredit the truth of her statements, but she stood by them, making him appear unkind. It'd been the opposite of what he'd been going for.

Bertram, one of the partners in his firm, had looked highly displeased from his seat behind the defense table. Brett had sat there next to Bertram in support of Troy, but his features had been twisted in so much discomfort that Troy knew he was in trouble. In growing desperation, he tried to come up with a different strategy. Typically, he had the jury eating out of the palm of his hand by now, but this particular jury had turned against him.

Late that night, he'd gone over to his client's home. He'd asked him about this small group of homeowners, and Paul had complained about them, telling Troy that their claims must be inaccurate. Then, in a last-ditch attempt at some leniency from the jury, Troy mentioned the idea of Paul's wife, Dynasty—yes, that was the woman's real name—going up on the stand. If she could demonstrate how grief-stricken her husband had been over the loss of his mother, maybe that would make for some wiggle room on their side of the aisle.

Dynasty had told her husband she didn't want to do that, but he ordered her to. That had led to a horrific screaming match between the two which Troy had been stuck in the middle of. Then, after Troy left, Paul had called, saying his wife had agreed to take the stand, but something about the whole thing felt iffy. Troy went ahead with his plan, though. What other option did he have?

During the next session when he called Dynasty up, he felt a chill skitter up his spine. His instincts were telling him to back off this line of questioning, but he was in too deep to do anything else now.

"Mrs. Adams, thank you for appearing today," Troy began. "Will you tell us what you know about your husband's state of mind during the block of time in question? Can you speak to how distraught he was over his mother's death?"

"Objection," the prosecuting attorney called out. "Relevance?"

"Your honor, I only wish to demonstrate that my client may have been briefly incapable of making rational decisions due to being emotionally compromised." Adams had been keen on this idea, which proved the dude was perfectly cognizant of what he'd done, but Troy had been left between a rock and a hard place.

The judge frowned, but then said, "Overruled. Continue, counselor. Mrs. Adams, please answer the question."

She nodded, then said, "Sure. He wasn't distraught at all."

Did the woman know what "distraught" even meant? Troy gave her his most patient half-grin. "I'm sorry. I must've misspoken. Can you tell us how upset he was?" This was Troy's final gambit.

"Like I said, he wasn't upset at all. He didn't get along with his mother and was happy to see her gone."

What the…

The court burst into a cacophony of noise. Everyone from the observing members of the media to the jury released gasps and sounds of surprise to the point that the judge was forced to pound his gavel and demand, "Order! Order in the court." Gradually, the commotion settled back down.

Troy blinked at Dynasty Adams, who was sitting on the stand with her chin pointed upwards and her face defiant. For the first time in his life, there he was in court, having no clue what to do.

"Mrs. Adams," the judge addressed her next. "Would you care to clarify what you just said?"

"Absolutely, your honor. My husband abandoned his mother in a nursing home years ago. He couldn't have cared less when she died, except that it meant he no longer had to pay for her care. And I'm sure he did rip off those homeowners. It's definitely something he would do."

"Dynasty!" Paul stood and shouted her name. "Why are you doing this?"

"Because it's the truth. I'm tired of hiding this, of pretending to be the blissful little family so you can look good for your business cronies. I'm over this and over you. I'm taking the girls and leaving this sham of a marriage."

The judge hit his gavel again, but it was too late. The damage had been done. Troy had glanced around him, feeling as if he'd been dropped into the center of a soap opera. How had this happened?

Later, when the jury made the ruling and found the defendant, Paul Adams, guilty, Troy stood by his client, feeling numb. All this had come totally out of left field, and Troy simply went through the motions after that. When the press bellowed out their numerous inquiries, he'd merely muttered, "No comment," over and over again. It'd been a nightmare of epic proportions.

The next day, when he was summoned into his firm's conference room, he'd entered knowing they'd be unhappy with how things had turned out but also expecting a modicum of compassion. Never in his life had a case blown up in his face so thoroughly, but it hadn't been his fault. None of the information he'd had hinted that his case would implode like a deep space star under its own gravitational pressure.

He felt chagrined, though. Maybe it could happen to anyone, but until then, it hadn't ever happened to him. He needed the support of his firm to help him feel better about all this. Bertram and Rockford were in attendance, but Brett was nowhere to be seen. Where was he?

"Mr. Sykes, I'll get straight to the point," Rockford said. "Based on your disappointing performance on such a significant and public case, the firm has decided to let you go. We need you to pack up your office and exit the building."

Shocked and dumbfounded, Troy asked, "What?"

"You're fired," Bertram spat, his jaw as hard as a rock. "Do you know how much damage your incompetence has caused to our firm's reputation over this? You should've done your homework and uncovered these issues before you went to trial, but you didn't. Now, your client's name has been tied to all of ours and our firm is being dragged through the mud all over the evening news."

"But, sir, I—"

"No," Bertram went on, a vein throbbing in his temple and his face the color of an overripe tomato. "Guerrero convinced us that you were ready. That you were better than this. Obviously, he was mistaken."

Troy stared at Bertram, flabbergasted. This couldn't be real. Was he having some sort of stress-related hallucination? Or maybe an out-of-body experience? He began to sweat profusely inside his suit, and his heart rate became so accelerated, he couldn't count the beats.

"You can't fire me right after hiring me," he blurted out. "Not when it wasn't my fault."

"Sure, we can," Bertram countered. "Your signing bonus came with the contingency that you win your first three cases."

Troy closed his eyes, seeing the information he'd skimmed over. He'd known it was there, but he'd been so certain he would, that he hadn't thought about it since then. They really did have the means to fire him, but he swayed people for a living.

"Give me a second chance, sir. I'll prove how good I can be to this firm."

"That ship has sailed, Sykes," Bertram barked out.

Then Rockford said, his voice almost kind now, "Go to your office and get yourself together. We'll send Guerrero along to help you load up your things."

That ship has sailed. Bertram's words drilled through his brain. But it couldn't have sailed. This was supposed to be his big opportunity. This was supposed to be the achievement that would allow him to make partner. And instead, they were giving him the boot?

It was then that some switch inside of Troy clicked, and he went from shock to sheer wrath at the injustice of it all. "The ship hasn't sailed. The case was a gong show, but I can't be blamed for that. I'm not leaving."

"Son," Rockford started, but Troy didn't let him speak.

"Don't you call me son. You want to fire me, but I'm not gonna let you."

Bertram's complexion darkened even further. "Now you've just lost the privilege of packing up. Get out. Get out now!"

At that, Troy lost it a little bit. Even though Rockford had been gentler with him than Bertram, it was Rockford he took a swing at. The room erupted as two beefy security guards flew through the door, came up on either side of Troy, and forcibly threw him out of the building.

Off balance, Troy stumbled and ended up falling down the cement steps, scraping his hand and wrenching his wrist along the way. Still livid, he rose to his feet, ready to tackle the security guards, when two police cars, sirens blaring and lights flashing, appeared at the curb. Before he knew it, he was handcuffed as they read him his Miranda rights, then placed in the back seat; he hadn't even heard or seen them coming.

Once arrested, he was patted down, fingerprinted, and photographed for his mug shot before being shunted into a holding cell. It was all a blur. He'd never been in any type of jail or incarceration facility except to see a client. It felt entirely different on this side of the bars. His anger kept simmering just below the surface, so it took him being an inmate for hours before he settled enough to engage the more logical side of his brain.

He knew he'd be arraigned soon. While technically he could represent himself, losing his freedom like this meant he'd have difficulty collecting the resources he needed to provide himself with a decent defense.

How ironic was that?

Brett would be the ideal candidate to be his attorney, but Troy didn't even know if his best friend was speaking to him. Had the firm given Brett the boot too, or did his status as a junior partner protect him? Now that he thought about it, he doubted they'd let Brett represent him due to the conflict of interest, anyway. Attempting to determine the correct course of action and coming up with a big fat goose egg, he welcomed seeing an officer stalk by his cell.

"What am I being held on?"

"Criminal trespass and assault and battery," the cop muttered, not even slowing his stride.

And Troy registered something. While he had a phone call coming to him, he didn't know who to contact. With Brett out of the running, that left his family, but he didn't want to reach out to either his mother or his sister. They believed in him, counted on him. Them hearing about all this made him feel nauseous.

Yet they would hear about this. Bertram and Rockford had told him the outcome of his trial was already all over the news, and based on the press hounding him and his client on the courthouse steps, he was certain that was true. Still, he needed to get out of here without involving anyone he knew. Finally, realization dawned.

A public defender.

He wasn't able to meet with him for another thirty-six hours, and by then, the torch of his hope had dwindled down to a smoldering flame about to die. Troy had barely slept since his cell had been filled with other men, and he couldn't lie down. His suit was not only wrinkled but torn from his altercation. To make matters worse, when he was escorted into the claustrophobic meeting room, the man waiting there for him appeared to be about twelve.

"Zachary Falstetter, public defender," the kid introduced himself. He was redheaded, freckled, and clean shaven.

"How old are you?" Troy asked brusquely, feeling belea-guered by this insane turn his path had taken. Had the county saddled him with someone who hadn't even obtained his law school degree or passed the bar yet? They couldn't have, right? That wouldn't be lawful.

"Twenty-seven," Zachary answered, his tone long-suffering enough that Troy understood he had to answer such queries often. "Now, what can you tell me about the circumstances of your situation?"

Troy explained the whole disaster and watched his lawyer absorb all the deets.

"The charges against you are both misdemeanors and since they're first offenses, the judge will likely fine you at your arraignment. Once you pay that fine, you'll be released."

"If I'm found guilty, you mean."

"Yes," Zachary spoke slowly. "You should know that there is security cam footage of you attempting to punch Mr. Rockford. There is also a video of you being arrested that's making its rounds with the media. It's gone viral." Then, the kid pulled out his phone and showed him. There were hashtags like #SuitEatsCement and #LawyerNeeds-ALawyer. There was no possible way he would be found not guilty. "Would you like to consider a plea deal?"

Troy stared at his defender, speechless. Regardless of the fact that he felt wronged by his former employers, he hadn't been born yesterday. He knew he didn't have a reliable leg to stand on. The arrest footage of him tumbling down the steps and struggling as the police cuffed him had hit over two million views already.

"Yeah," he said, resigned as he rubbed at his sore wrist. "I'm willing to look at a plea deal."

Events followed a predictable pattern after that. After Zachary let him borrow a comb—they'd taken the one Troy always carried—some spray deodorant, and a travel-size bottle of mouthwash, they went together before the judge. Troy had stood in front of a judge so many times, but never like this. It felt degrading to be brought before the court in such a manner.

By pleading guilty to the assault and battery charge, the judge dropped the criminal trespassing for refusal to leave charge. It meant his sentence added up to two thousand dollars rather than twenty-five hundred, but beggars couldn't be choosers. But as humiliating as being declared a criminal felt, he still had to reach out to someone to provide the money that would ensure his release.

And since only one person fit that bill, this might prove to be more difficult still.

CHAPTER SEVEN

THE LAST TIME SHE'D EXPERIENCED A BREAKUP WITH TROY, she'd gone through the stages of grief in a much different manner. Back at UTEP, she'd stayed in denial for days. She'd suppressed her anger so she could spend the next week bargaining with God to send Troy back to her—talk about pathetic. It'd taken her a month of debilitating depression and lots more tears than she'd ever want to admit before she'd been able to finally accept the truth of the situation. It'd been a long and painful journey.

This time, however, had been remarkably different. She'd started and finished with denial prior to their discussion even concluding. She'd skipped right over bargaining because the man quite frankly wasn't worth it. She hadn't felt depressed because she'd boiled with fury. Amber had already accepted what had transpired. That wasn't the problem.

The problem was that she couldn't seem to go long without her ire materializing like a hideous beast from some old monster movie to reap annihilation on either her belongings or her peace of mind.

To date, she'd broken a plastic spatula, cut her thumb while picking up the remainder of her bathroom mirror, and stubbed her toe. Her emotions had been vacillating between this simmering resentment to an incensed and violent outrage for the better part of a week now. Those episodic explosions were responsible not only for the damage done to her phone, but also to every item she'd received from the ex that shall no longer be named.

And yes, while he was due a heaping helping of that fury —he'd earned it, after all—she saved the lion's share for herself. How had she let this happen? How had she allowed a man she'd known to be untrustworthy sneak the wool over her eyes *for a second time*? She felt like someone being told not to touch that electric fence and grasping onto it anyway. For the love of *snow cones*, how much of a glutton for punishment could she be?

What infuriated her the most was how the man had managed to blindside her when such a thing should've been inconceivable. She should have suspected him of being disingenuous, to return to his selfish and narcissistic habits. He'd already shown her his true colors once, but she'd wanted to believe him capable of more. She'd liked him, or at least the idea of him, so she kept overlooking his flaws so she could bestow attributes on him he didn't possess.

Attributes like decency. Honesty. Compassion. Understanding. The ability to love.

Needing to pinpoint his issues with unflinching precision, she sat at her office desk and looked up the term narcissism on her laptop, which was necessary since she was having the shattered screen on her phone replaced. While she'd taken some rudimentary level psych courses, it hadn't been her focus, so she felt the desire to corroborate what she thought she remembered.

Narcissism was more common in men. Big surprise. Narcissists tended to feel entitled to get whatever they wanted and do whatever they pleased. Yep. They felt a compulsion to be admired and revered. Bingo. They may disregard the feelings of others.

Oh, you think?

Grace came into her office then, a large Starbucks Frappuccino in one hand and a black and white bag labeled the Geek Squad in her other. "What'd you say?"

Great, Amber must've said that last bit out loud. "Nothing. One of those for me?"

"Both, actually."

"Have I told you how amazing you are?"

"No, but I already know," her bestie answered cheekily. Yet once Amber collected her repaired phone and took a swig of her Frap, she felt her friend's eyes on her. It grated more than it probably should've, and before she knew it, Amber snapped.

"If you're here to stare at me like a tiger in a cage, feel free to leave."

"Ah, there she is. Dr. Amber Crawford, otherwise known as Little Miss Sunshine. And, by the way, you're welcome," Grace deadpanned, looking at her askance. Amber huffed out a long breath. Then, she took in another and exhaled slowly again.

"I'm sorry, Gracie. I truly am. I've been crabbier than a crabapple, haven't I?"

"Oh yeah," her bestie told her baldly, refusing to sugarcoat things.

"Sorry," she apologized for the second time in less than a minute.

"Amber, I get it. A man broke your trust. It hurts, and it makes you mad. But stomping around the birthing ward like Yosemite Sam on a tirade isn't ultimately going to help. You know that, right?"

Amber sighed. "I suppose I do."

"Missy Smith's preeclampsia is under control, and Holly Brubarb is remarkably healthy for a forty-five-year-old in her third trimester."

"You took Missy and Holly?" Those two mamas-to-be were each patients of Amber's and somehow, she hadn't even absorbed that they were there that day. *Good job taking care of those you're responsible for, Amber. Way to go.*

"Don't worry about it," Grace said, waving a dismissive hand in the air, but Amber couldn't dismiss it. Her issues with her recent breakup were negatively impacting the care she provided her patients, and she couldn't allow that to continue.

"No, I *am* going to worry about it. I need to be doing my job, not hulking out in my office."

Grace released a noise somewhere between a chortle and a snort. "If you really do turn green and hulk out, please holler at me. This I got to see."

"Rude," Amber declared, pinching her upper arm.

"I'm not rude. I'm an angel."

"Yeah, right."

They both burst out giggling then, which relieved much of the tension. She didn't think she'd laughed since her ex had pulled his nonsense. Yet, the moment he entered her consciousness, her levity evaporated.

Whether the man was truly a certifiable narcissist or not, he'd tricked her. He'd played games with her heart, then cruelly thrown it up against the wall, destroying the organ while it was still beating. It'd been seven days, and she felt almost as ransacked by it as the day it'd happened. She didn't feel like she'd healed at all and wished she had an ETA on when she would.

Good luck with that.

Regardless, though, it was time to cowgirl up. If she didn't, it would not only be unprofessional, it would mean that she let the ex who shall no longer be named win. Grace's phone buzzed and she glanced at it, stealing a surreptitious look at Amber narrowing her gaze back at her cell.

"Everything okay?"

"Peachy," Grace frowned. "Dave just texted me with the good news that our babysitter has tonsillitis, and she apparently received this news after she was already there and probably infecting our daughter." Grace's daughter, Samantha, was a year old. "And he's stuck at the airport because his flight is delayed."

"Why'd she text Dave when he's out of town?"

"I don't know," she sounded exasperated. "Dave keeps saying the girl is scared of me, and—" Before her friend felt compelled to explain whatever all that might entail, Amber cut her off.

"Go. I'll hold down the fort here."

"You sure?" her BFF asked her, but she was already treading backward out the door.

"Of course. It'll be fine. I hope Samantha feels better."

"Thanks," Grace called out as she hurried away.

In actuality, her bestie's departure turned out to be a blessing. Amber stayed too busy for the rest of her shift to stop moving, which meant she didn't have the time or energy to dwell on her two-time ex. That night when she arrived home, she took a long, hot shower and then sort of just oozed her tired self into bed early. Fortunately, she'd be off the following day.

Her phone rang, and she grabbed at it, feeling as if she'd just drifted off. She couldn't have, though, because sunlight poured in through the slim gap in her curtains, making a stripe of white across the throw rugs decorating the hardwood of her bedroom floor. "Hello?"

"Forget something?"

"Daddy?" she vaulted up to a seated position. "What's wrong?"

"Did I wake you?"

"Um, maybe a little."

He chuckled at her. "Must've had a difficult day yesterday." A difficult week, actually, but who was counting? She heard noise in the background. The scraping of utensils on plates and people chattering. "I take it you won't be meeting me here for breakfast, then?"

Breakfast at the Waffle House. *Snow cones*! How could she have forgotten that? Customarily, she set her alarm so she'd be sure to be up and at 'em when her dad asked her out for a meal, but she'd been so exhausted last night that she hadn't. Not that she could tell her dad that. He wasn't even aware that she'd rekindled things with her nefarious ex in the first place. Which was good because while Jeff Crawford saved lives for a living, when it came to protecting his only child, he had a pretty gnarly temper.

Maybe that was where Amber got hers from.

"I'm so sorry, Daddy. Let me get dressed and I'll—"

"Nope. You sound bushed. Go back to bed." He paused a second. "It is just fatigue, right? You're not sick or anything, are you?"

"No, not sick. Just wiped out."

"Okay. We'll reschedule for another day, then. See you soon, precious."

She'd set down her phone for maybe thirty seconds, closing her eyes and burying her face in her pillow, when it rang again.

"Daddy?" she murmured, keeping her eyes shut as she brought her cell to her mouth.

"This is the El Paso County Detention Facility," came a woman's rough and unfamiliar voice. Amber blinked her eyelids open immediately. "Will you accept a collect call from inmate Troy Sykes?"

"Excuse me?" she asked, needing to hear a repeat of the request that made not one lick of sense. Maybe she'd fallen all the way back to sleep and was groggier than she thought.

"This is the El Paso County Detention Facility." The operator spoke each word at a higher volume and with more explicit deliberation. "Will you accept a collect call from inmate Troy Sykes?"

Amber reclined there, tucked between her sheets as she gaped at the meadow-green walls of her bedroom. Then, she pushed herself into a seated position. Was this some sort of prank? Had someone volunteered her house as a filming location for some outlandish reality show? And more to the point, if it truly was her ex on the other end of the line, should she even deign to answer?

CHAPTER EIGHT

TROY WAITED ON TENTERHOOKS FOR AMBER TO AGREE TO TAKE his call. She would agree, wouldn't she? He loathed the truth of this, but she was his last lifeline. He'd been too wound up to eat and was tired since he had nowhere to sleep. And despite Zachary letting him freshen up by the slightest degree, he felt like he'd spent the previous two days living in some filthy dumpster.

Since he hadn't asked to contact anyone until after his arraignment and sentencing, they'd taken his suit and fancy leather dress shoes and told him to change into a neon orange prison jumpsuit and cheap slip-on shoes he typically wouldn't be caught dead in. He'd been put—and had put himself—through nine levels of indignity by delaying things for this long. He regretted that now. Which was why he felt so eager for Amber to answer.

"Ma'am," he heard the operator speak up again. "You are not required to take this call. If you don't wish to accept the charges, you can either say no or simply hang up."

Troy's lungs did this perplexing aching thing. It felt as if someone had taken his collection of law books and stacked every last one of them on his chest.

"Um… I guess I will."

Thank all that was good and holy. "Am, I have a favor to ask."

"You've got some nerve," she growled at him. Wow. He'd never heard her growl before. "Calling me up after what you did. And from the county jail, no less."

"I'm not overly thrilled about the prospect either," he ground out, his aggravation rearing up without warning again. But he squashed it. He needed her to help him, and you won more flies with honey, after all. "Sorry. But I really did plan to get back together with you as soon as I won the trial."

A ringing silence followed this sentence, and it occurred to him that he wasn't coming across as well as he wanted to. Up until recently, communication skills had been his forte. Troy was so off his game. If he had any chance of her helping him out, he'd probably have to grovel to accomplish it, which was fine. He'd never had a problem with saying whatever might be needed to make things go his way.

"I shouldn't have broken us up again. I get it."

"Do you get it, Troy? Do you really? Because I sincerely doubt that." He could hear her huffing and puffing as if she'd been doing fifty-yard sprints.

He cut to the chase. "I need your help. I've gotten involved in some... legal entanglements. I need you to pay my fine, so I can get out. Then, if you can give me a ride home..."

A peal of derisive hysteria interrupted him then, but nothing about her laughter struck him as mirthful.

"I'll pay you back, Am. I promise," he told her, thinking maybe that would do the trick, but she barreled off on a tangent as if he hadn't spoken.

"Why have you designated me as the person to handle this? Thanks to you, we're not a couple anymore, remember?"

"It's a long story."

"How convenient for you," her words hit him like icicles, and it set him off again.

"No, it's not convenient for me. My career has crashed and burned, my professional reputation is in the gutter, and I'm *incarcerated*, Amber. I've gone from hotshot lawyer to having a criminal record for the rest of my life. Don't you understand how hard this is for me?"

He hadn't meant to say all that, he'd meant to apologize in such a way that she'd assist him, but somehow, he'd gone utterly off the rails again. He felt pain shoot through his injured wrist, and he peered at it, registering that he'd clenched that hand into a fist. He flexed his fingers, making those muscles relax, and the pain lessened. Why did all of these terrible things keep happening to him, one right after the other? Troy felt rattled and not like himself. And every attempt he made to remedy things kept backfiring on him.

She cursed under her breath, something he didn't remember her ever doing prior to now.

"You do realize that I have every reason in the universe to despise the fact that you even exist, don't you?" She spouted that out like a rhetorical question, so he didn't answer. "I may regret this later, but I suppose I should do it. For me, though. Not you. I believe in being a good person and doing the right thing, even when people don't deserve it."

"So you'll get me out?" he asked, just to clarify.

"I will."

Relief burst below his sternum and rose up to fill his chest.

"But only on one condition," she amended, and he knew he'd meet it. If he stayed behind bars much longer, he'd go legitimately crazy.

"Name it."

"After I pay your fine and drop you off at your place, you'll be gone from my life forever. No more texts. No more calls. No more comic strips. No more stops and starts. If we happen to bump into each other here in town, we'll pretend to be strangers. I never want you to darken my doorstep again. You hear me?"

Stunned by the vitriol in her tone, he shoved a hand through his unwashed hair. "I hear you."

"I mean it, Troy," she doubled down, as if she could hear something false in his tone.

"Yeah, I can tell," he told her, and this time, he didn't say it to get her to comply with his wishes. He understood that she was cutting ties permanently.

"So you agree to those terms without question?"

"I agree."

He waited for her to say something else, even if that something was hateful, but it wasn't Amber's voice he heard next. "She's no longer on the line," the operator said as dispassionately as if she were staring at paint as it dried. Then, with the clank of a landline headset, she hung up. The operator had listened to their entire call, which reminded him that while he was trapped in this place, he'd have zero privacy. Man, he couldn't get out of there fast enough.

A guard nudged him, and Troy pivoted, letting the man lead him back to the holding cell. A couple of boys who he wasn't even certain were of age goggled back at him, horror in their expressions. He didn't know why they were in there or what they had done. Troy turned away, telling himself he didn't care. Yet, when his name was called an hour later, he caught sight of each of them a second time, their complexions pale and terrified.

Over the next hour, he was processed out. A uniformed officer gave back his belongings. Troy retrieved his dress shirt, tie, slacks, and suit jacket, hurrying to yank them on despite how bad they looked and smelled. Amber stood there in the corridor once he finished, her eyes stone-like and staring straight ahead. When she hurried out, he followed her, staying right on her heels. They didn't speak as they strode to her Audi, and not once did she even glimpse in his direction as they left the detention facility together.

The ride to his place didn't take long, but the hostility level inside her SUV was as thick as pea soup. Yet, that didn't matter. All that mattered was that he'd soon be home, and once there, he could clean up, rest, and ferret out what to do next. She screeched to a halt in his circle drive, waiting for him to open the passenger's side door and step out. While it was still cracked wide, he turned to her, scrutinizing her profile. She'd held up her end of the bargain, and now, he'd hold up his. Even if for some reason, imagining her going made him feel hollow.

"Hey, Am?"

"What?" she grunted out.

"Thanks."

She said nothing in return. He pushed the door shut and took a pace back. She gunned the engine, zooming around his driveway. He watched as her Audi braked at the intersection before tearing out of sight.

Amber hadn't looked back at him. Not even once.

Being back inside the confines of his luxury home was a comfort, but not as much of one as he'd thought. He scrubbed and scrubbed at his skin while under his fancy shower nozzle, but even after staying in there until all the hot water was gone, he didn't feel totally clean. After drying off, he threw on some flannel pants and a tee and skidded onto his mattress. But even though he felt worn out to the point of his eyes being gritty, he didn't nod off.

Lying there on his back, his head filled with disturbing images of the events of the past two days. Brett hanging his head in disappointment. Bertram shouting at him. Rockford springing back from Troy's punch. His public defender's blank expression as he told Troy they couldn't win. The fear on those boys' faces in the holding cell. The rigid coldness of Amber's posture as he studied her profile.

Despite his perfectly firm mattress and twelve-hundred-thread-count sheets, he couldn't get comfortable.

Troy bounded confidently into the courtroom where Amber sat on the stand. He asked her questions which she answered readily, a smile on her face. But then, her features altered. Her brows furrowed as she narrowed her eyes at him, her lips forming a taut line. When she spoke up again, he couldn't understand her —it was as if she were speaking another language. Then, she began to repeat herself at a shout, until finally, what she said made sense.

"You're a horrible person, Troy Sykes, and I hate you!"

Gasping, he woke, his heart galloping like an unbroken stallion. Perspiration covered him from head to foot as he absorbed that it had just been a dream. His muscles almost relaxed as comprehension dawned. While it had been a dream, Amber did hate him. Of that he was sure.

Switching to his right side, Troy stared into the darkness of his room, feeling that hollow sensation from earlier growing.

CHAPTER NINE

AMBER PADDED OVER TO THE NURSERY WARD, PORING OVER the faces of the twins she'd delivered a few hours previous. They were fraternal twins, a boy and a girl, both of whom were napping with their thumbs in their mouths. She adored observing babies, especially when they were sound asleep. She loved how carefree they were, their tiny faces in repose. She traced her index finger along the girl's smooth forehead, surprised when her brother was the one to lift his pale lashes and nearly translucent eyelids into awareness.

The little fellow's eyes were a vibrant blue, and she stared at him, reminded of Troy. Her ex's eyes were a similar hue, the kind that stood out and made people take notice, but then she chastised herself. Why had that comparison popped into her head? The man was the scummiest of scumbags and she wanted nothing to do with him. She'd erased him from her phone and blocked his number, an act she knew was the best not only for her heart, but for her sanity.

Waiting for the baby to slip into a delicate snooze again, she trudged back out, careful to make no noise. She'd just tugged the windowed door shut when she peeked up to find Grace so close she almost knocked her over.

"*Snow cones*," she hissed, keeping her voice down even though her best friend had startled her half out of her gourd.

"You're as skittish as a colt," Grace joked, but then the curve of her lips drooped. "Are you okay?"

"Fine." Her friend pursed her mouth as if she didn't believe her but let her be.

The morning after she'd dropped off her ex, she'd received a PayPal notification alerting her a deposit would be added to her account. It'd been the money he'd owed her plus fifty bucks. Maybe it was to cover the little bit of gas she'd used or to cover the PayPal fee, but she didn't plan to question it. She needed her door to be shut on him from now on.

Since she'd missed a planned meal with her father, she made sure she kept their next scheduled slot intact. As she walked into the Waffle House and breathed in the aromas of pancake batter, syrup, eggs, and bacon, she spotted her dad in their usual corner booth. She caught sight of him before he did her, and something about his tight expression made her study him more closely. Then, as soon as he saw her, he smiled at her, his features sliding into their usual configuration.

"Precious, how are you?"

"Good, Daddy. How are you?" She maintained eye contact as she asked this, curious as to what he might say.

"Good, but uh…" He averted his gaze from her face and down to the tabletop. "I have something I need to tell you."

Instantly, worst-case scenarios filled all the blanks inside her head. Was he ill? Had he gotten laid off? Was he losing his house? Was he dying? Was it possible to have a heart attack at the age of twenty-nine?

"Whoa, precious, calm down. You just went as white as a sheet. It's not bad news, I promise."

Still, she couldn't keep from feeling skeptical about that. If it wasn't bad, why did he look like he was about to swallow his own tongue?

Before he could elaborate, a server approached dressed in her blue, button-down shirt and long, black apron. "What can I get for you fine folks?"

"I'd like coffee to drink, and the cheese and eggs with raisin toast," Amber answered, reciting her regular order.

"Coffee for me too," her dad ordered next. "And the steak and eggs with the hash browns smothered in grilled onions to keep it healthy." He glanced over at his daughter with a twinkle in his eye. This was their perpetual joke. Though they both attempted to eat nutritionally sound meals day to day, they both cheated joyfully during their bi-weekly or once a month Waffle House breakfasts.

But once the server left, Amber was reminded of their original discussion. She held her hands under the table, lacing them together in her lap. Pasting what she hoped was an innocuous look on her face, she asked, "Okay, what is it?"

"Well, I..." He scratched at the back of his neck as if he had an itchy tag. "I met someone."

Amber quit breathing as she waited for the other shoe to drop. "Uh huh."

"And I like her. I really like her. We've been dating."

Her dad had been dating? How had she not known this?

"Who is it?"

"Patti Kendall."

"Oh, the new librarian?"

His lips twitched into a smile. "The same."

"How long has this been going on?"

"Three months, more or less. We were keeping things light, but recently, we've discovered that we have feelings that run more deeply than that. Now that things are more serious, I want you to know about her, to meet her."

She'd only seen Patti Kendall in passing, but she seemed nice from what Amber could tell.

"All right."

"Are you upset?" he asked next.

"Why would I be upset?"

"Well, because I haven't dated another woman since your mother. Partly because I was concentrating on raising you and partly because I wanted to honor your mom's memory." He still seemed so nervous and on edge. "I didn't know how you'd feel about it."

"I feel fine about it," she said, meaning it. "Mom's been gone for nearly three decades, Daddy. I'd say it's okay if you want to move on." There'd been more than once when she'd worried about him being lonely. It was a wonder he hadn't done this sooner. Still, he seemed awfully tentative about the whole thing.

"Yeah?"

"Yeah. I want you to be happy. And I know I get all mired down in my work sometimes. It'd be nice for you to have someone else to turn to. Not that I'll ever stop being here for you, but—"

"I know, precious girl." He chuckled. "It's not that we aren't taking our time or plan to exchange rings at the JP's or anything, but this feels real. I kind of think we have a chance to make it for the long haul."

"That's fabulous, Daddy, really. And I'm looking forward to being properly introduced."

His posture slumped a little and he closed his eyes, displaying just how tied in knots he'd been over this. Silly man. Didn't he know all she wanted for him was joy and contentment? And if that meant a lifelong companion, so much the better.

"That's a load off my shoulders. I've been trying to fritter out how I could tell you."

She pulled her hands out from under the table so she could grasp his fingers in hers. "I was being honest before. I'm thrilled that you're endeavoring to branch out like that romantically, and I'd love to get to know her." He squeezed her fingers back.

"Now that I'm finally branching out, as you say, what are we going to do about you?"

Amber jerked her chin up, startled. "What about me?"

He blinked at her with his broad, familiar smile. "You just sang the praises of me getting out into the dating world. When are you going to do the same?"

"Why? Is this your way of asking for grandchildren?" she teased, but his reply surprised her.

"I wouldn't be disappointed by the pitter patter of little grandbaby feet."

He'd never once mentioned such a thing till now. She decided to handle it with as much levity as she could muster.

"Didn't you always tell me I couldn't date till I was thirty-five? I still have six years to go, you know."

The server brought their food, and her dad tapped on his plate with the tines of his fork. "I find it a bit concerning that you haven't dated since that boy back in college, that's all. Not that I don't want you to be selective, because I do, but you have so much to offer."

The only part of that paragraph she heard was "that boy back in college." If only he knew. Which, of course, he wouldn't. Not if she could help it.

"So you do want grandchildren," was her weak attempt at deflection.

"I'm sure they'd be fun. But that's not why I brought this up. You said you want me happy, so I'm reflecting that message right back at you. I'm not going to be around forever."

Amber shuddered inwardly. No one knew better than her the fragility of life. How easily and quickly it could be taken. Growing up, she had countless nightmares about losing her dad. Partly because of his firefighting and partly because the only memory she had of her mother was visiting her grave. Life was a flame that could at any moment be snuffed out.

"Daddy, please don't."

"I'm only pointing out the truth. I know you're a modern woman with a topnotch education and an even more topnotch career. I'm so proud of you I could burst. But I don't like thinking of you spending your entire life alone."

"You basically did." The words were out of her mouth before she could stop them, but this topic of conversation was knocking her off kilter.

"I had you," he countered softly. "So I stayed plenty occupied. I may not be much of a public speaker or anything, but what I'm trying to say is that life isn't made up of only a single road. There are lots of side trails, so I'd like to encourage you to check out a few. The one thing I don't want you to do is wake up one morning at ninety years old and realize that you wished you'd hopped off the interstate more often. That's all."

Rarely did she and her dad speak like this, and it was making her eyes feel hot and prickly. "I hear you, Captain Crawford. Loud and clear." She didn't want to tell him that due to that ex, she'd pretty much given up on romance. Shining the spotlight back on him, she asked, "So, how'd you wind up dating Patti?"

"On eHarmony."

"What?" she laughed. "Seriously? Your firehouse and the library where she works are literally a few blocks away from each other."

"Yeah, but I wanted to find a woman who wasn't just cute but a match, as they say." He shrugged. "Why roll the dice on some random blind date when I can get to see what I can expect through a woman's profile?"

She shook her head at him. "I can't believe you're just now telling me about all this." Then, she felt guilty for saying it. Apparently, they'd each had secrets the other didn't know, despite how close they'd always been.

"Eh, I'm fifty-eight, not eighty. I don't like to think of myself as an old fogey. I can be as modern as the next fella."

To be honest, it felt a little disconcerting to look at Jeff Crawford as a man who had an interest in not being left all by his lonesome anymore in addition to being her father. Nonetheless, they'd both been adults for a long time. She reached across the narrow table and squeezed his wrist affectionately.

"I'll consider some side trails. Also, I love you very much."

"Love you too, precious."

CHAPTER TEN

TROY WOKE TO THE SOUND OF HIS DOORBELL BLARING through his home, and he considered not answering it due to how annoying it was to have a visitor at six in the morning. Forcing himself to shift off his mattress and throwing on a robe, he shuffled down his stairs, feeling grumpy. His sleep-addled brain told him maybe someone was delivering something he'd find useful in his job search, even though the logic of that notion failed him.

It wasn't as if anyone was knocking down the door of the infamous #LawyerNeedsALawyer with job offers. And it wasn't for lack of looking for another position either.

Once he opened his door, he found a young guy with a beard wearing a dress shirt, khakis, and loafers. "Can I help you?" Troy asked him.

"Uh, hi there… Are you Troy Sykes?" Khakis asked in a timid voice.

"That's me."

"Excellent," Khakis' voice became much firmer as he handed Troy one of those large, dark yellow envelopes. "Consider yourself served."

Troy frowned. "Served with what?" But Khakis was already jogging off down Troy's steps to the car parked by the fountain next to his circle drive. He opened the envelope to see something familiar: a summons.

Official Subpoena from the State of Texas, the County of El Paso:

The Civil District Attorney hereby requires that Troy Sykes appear before the court at **9:00 a.m. on August 15th** *pursuant to a claim of Defamation of Character brought before the court by plaintiffs Stanley Bertram and Trent Rockford of the law firm Bertram and Rockford.*

176.B Enforcement of Subpoena: *(a)* **Contempt**. *Failure by any person to obey a subpoena appearance request may be deemed a contempt of the district court of the county in which it is served and may be punishable by fine, confinement, or both.*

Troy read over the document three consecutive times in shocked disbelief. Not only was he unemployed, he now also faced whatever bogus charge his former employers had dreamed up. Just when he thought the worst was over, some other nasty issue would crop up.

Other than a few "I'm fine; these are just some minor setbacks," text replies to the frantic calls he'd received from Mia and his mother, he hadn't communicated with them. He'd even pretended not to be home when they'd come by. He couldn't face either of them—or reach out to Brett—until he had another job, proving to them that he'd overcome his current set of obstacles.

This summons added a whole new set to his already heavy load, so he went to his home gym. Inside was a weightlifting set, a stationary bike, a rowing machine, and a treadmill. Dropping his subpoena on a table by the door, he bounded up onto the treadmill and started a punishing workout that included steep hills and speeds that kept increasing until the cooldown. By the time he stepped off the thing, his body felt looser and his head clearer.

He'd been fired unfairly, and he could make a judge see that through his sworn testimony. None of what had happened with Adams was Troy's fault, and if Bertram and Rockford hadn't provoked him, he never would've taken that swing in the first place. Despite being sent to jail, he still felt this whole travesty had been a massive misunderstanding. He'd just explain to the judge his side of things, and everything would get straightened out.

He knew it would. It *had* to be.

THREE WEEKS LATER, Troy sat on his sectional in a daze. Nothing had been straightened out. Worse, the judge had gone along with his former employers' side of the story and had declared a judgment against him. He glanced down at the sentencing paperwork in his hands. Bertram and Rockford must've had this judge in their pocket or something because he'd awarded the firm over nine hundred million dollars.

How was that amount even allowed?

Based on how absurdly over the top that sentence was, Troy appealed it, only for the judgment to be upheld, which meant he'd incurred even more fees. Instead of solving his problems, fighting for himself had only made things worse, and now he would lose the vast majority of the fortune he'd spent his career in California accumulating.

How had all this happened? He kept expecting to be shaken awake and for someone to tell him it'd all been a brutal nightmare. He couldn't wrap his mind around how bad everything in his life had become. It was as if he'd been skiing down a pristine slope up in Colorado like a gold medalist, only to faceplant into a tree right at the end. Before this, Troy hadn't thought so much could go so wrong all at once.

Yet, here he was, a living example that it could.

The court ruled that the amount he owed would be extracted out of his accounts, so in the space of a single day, his personal coffers went from overflowing to practically empty. In the end, he was left with the bare minimum required to keep his savings accounts active and a dramatically reduced number in his checking account. He'd gone from wealthy billionaire to essentially destitute overnight.

Even since he began making money hand over fist, Troy had spent it freely. He had all his bills automatically drafted out of his account and had a variety of fun stuff designed to operate in the same way. He had monthly subscriptions to gaming platforms and streaming services. He had mystery boxes delivered on a regular basis full of things like Marvel and DC comic book collectibles and the like.

It took him about a month before he comprehended that he needed to cancel all these superfluous expenses. And by then, a chunk of what had remained in his account had been spent. Because he'd financed his home with a mortgage rather than buying it outright, he had a massive payment every month. He panicked when he saw that within six months, he would no longer be capable of paying it.

Troy put his house on the market the next day, then began to sell his belongings. He started with the stuff that held no real importance, but once he realized that wouldn't be enough, went through things that were less easy to get rid of. By the time his house sold—which didn't net him much since he still owed the majority of the loan—he'd sold his exercise equipment and all but one of his vehicles.

He went through his belongings piece by piece, trying to come up with enough to afford somewhere else nice to live, but it wasn't meant to be. He'd agreed to vacate the property, but since he had nowhere else to go, he moved into a hotel. The hotel proved to be too expensive, so the next week, he moved to a Motel 6.

Even though he didn't want to, he considered moving out of state, but since the story had been seen not just locally but nationally, he didn't think it would work. Since he still had possession of his Hummer but couldn't afford the payments, he sold it and bought a used twelve-year-old

Ford Taurus outright. At least if he was kicked out of the motel, he could sleep in his car.

Within six months of the conclusion of the Adams case, the only possessions Troy still had were his phone, five of his suits, one pair of dress shoes, a handful of casual clothing, that Taurus, and what was left of his pride. More desperate for funds than he'd ever been in his life, he created a teaching course online, but it made him less than a hundred bucks a month.

To conceal just how much of a wreck he'd become, he'd straight up lied to his mom and sister, telling them that he'd moved back to California for a job there. He'd talked to them over the phone in this overly jolly voice, and even went so far as to take misleading pics of himself living it up. Dwindling into a shadow of his former self, Troy sat in his motel room on his lumpy bed, knowing that unless something changed, he'd have to move into his car within three days.

In order to keep from taking the last step into homelessness, he did the one thing he'd promised he wouldn't. He opened the contact list on his phone, his finger hovering over her number. Then, aware he was breaking his word, he called Amber. It barely rang once before her voicemail picked up.

"You have reached 915-555-8880, please leave a message after the beep." Then, a short beep sounded in his ear.

This struck him as peculiar, so he didn't leave a message. That wasn't the voicemail that Amber had previously. For someone else, changing the content of their message wouldn't be that big of a deal, but Amber had hers set up to receive messages from her patients. He knew she wouldn't give up being an obstetrician, so he checked the number. It was correct. He called her again even though he'd memorized the message. Was the beep shorter than it used to be? Why?

Rather than leave a voicemail, he sat there for a moment. Amber had been seriously upset at him the last time he'd seen her. Thinking about her made his chest ache, so he usually went out of his way to not think about her, but now, he had to.

He typed out a text and hit send. He received a message that said it was sent, but that was all. Since he was an attorney, he had his texts set up to visibly display which messages were delivered so he could use that in court if it ever became necessary. But Amber's phone never sent back a "delivered" message. He Googled what happened when someone blocked their calls, and it matched everything he'd just seen.

He guessed he shouldn't have been surprised.

The ache in his chest intensified, though. To his knowledge, he'd never been blocked before. That wasn't very considerate of her. Didn't she realize how demoralizing finding this out would be for him?

Taking a quick shower, he dressed in a pair of jeans and a T-shirt, got into his Taurus, and headed to her house. Only after arriving did he think about the fact that it was the middle of a weekday. Amber wouldn't be here, she'd be at the hospital. He felt disgusted by himself for not comprehending that earlier. What had he been thinking?

Something under his hood made a squealing noise as he headed in the direction of the Le Mesa Medical Center. Since he wasn't a car guy, all he could do was pray this old sedan would remain drivable. He continued onwards, the high-pitched sound plaguing him the entire trip.

CHAPTER ELEVEN

AMBER PEERED OUT HER WINDOW ON THE FOURTH FLOOR AND smiled. Snow. El Paso was one of those places where winter weather should be enjoyed because it could well be melted by the next day. She'd known weeks when there had been sleet and snow on Monday, rain on Tuesday, and a sixty-eight-degree high on Wednesday with no evidence that the snow or sleet had ever fallen.

Such was life so close to the Mexican border in the Lone Star state.

She gazed out at the mountain range during a slow time between appointments. When she'd been young, her dad had taken her hiking out there. They'd had a great time, but she hadn't been there in years. She kept telling herself she should take some time and go do it, yet there seemed to always be something else to do that was more important. Grace had instructed her to travel more too. But Amber never did.

Maybe this spring, she finally would.

She had taken a drink from her water bottle when she saw a tall figure crossing the parking lot. Amber wouldn't have thought anything of it—groups of people wandered around the hospital grounds throughout the day—but this person had golden blond hair and a masculine walk that she recognized. She frowned, squinting her eyes. The partly cloudy skies kept casting the occupants below into brightness and then shadow, making her wonder if maybe what she'd witnessed had been an optical illusion.

The man continued his trek toward the entrance, and she went motionless, not wanting him to spot her. It was either her ex or a look-alike, and since he wasn't a twin, that meant one thing. He was here. Her next impulse was to flee, which irritated her to the nth degree. He shouldn't be able to chase her off like bunny in her yard first thing in the morning. If he'd come to speak with her, she'd face him.

Then she'd tell him where he could go next. Which would be somewhere discernibly warmer than south Texas.

Every time the elevator dinged down the hallway, Amber found herself whipping her head around to look in that direction. She wanted to be prepared. She'd told the man off six months ago, and she didn't know why he might've decided to break the rules she'd set. In her mind, there was no statute of limitations. When she'd told him she never wanted to see him again, she'd meant it.

Besides, it would interrupt her day. Even if that particular day had been quiet so far.

And then, there he was. Unlike the last time he'd come into the maternity ward, his hands remained empty. He hadn't preceded his entrance by sending chocolate-covered cherries or bouquets of lilacs. Not that she'd accept them either way, but if he hoped to butter her up, he sure wasn't starting off on the right foot.

His head swiveled back and forth until he found her, and she braced herself for whatever nonsense he might plan to spout. He wore faded blue jeans, boots, and a jacket, and it annoyed her to notice that he'd remained as handsome as always. It seemed cardinally unfair for him to be so gorgeous. Wasn't that false advertising? The man should be forced to wear a warning sign on his chest.

Beware: Don't let the good looks fool you. I'm not the boyfriend material my face purports me to be.

The thought made her grin sardonically, so that was the expression she wore when their eyes met. The second his baby blues lined up with her hazel ones, she felt furious all over again. Who did this man think he was, anyway? He couldn't offer her anything in the galaxy that would make her return to him. Didn't he know that?

"Hey, Am," he said, halting in his tracks and thrusting his hands in his jacket pockets, a jacket that was too light for this weather.

She crossed her arms over her chest. "What are you doing here?"

"I, uh…" he trailed off, and she realized that they couldn't have this conversation out here on the floor, even if it wasn't busy.

"Come on." Amber grabbed his arm and dragged him over to her office, carefully shutting the door. He went along without offering her any resistance. "So, what? You forgot our deal, I suppose?"

"No, I didn't forget." He kept his voice low. "I just don't have any alternative."

"That's what you're going with? Being as smart as you are, I anticipated you coming up with something cleverer."

He stared at some invisible spot over her left shoulder. "This isn't some made-up story. I've lost everything, and you're my only hope."

She snorted at that, but it was humorless, an ugly sound.

"Right. Don't tell me your family has abandoned you. They wouldn't do that."

When she'd dated him, he'd talked about how much his mother and sister looked up to him. He'd acted as if they believed he could do no wrong. They'd never kick their beloved and revered Troy to the curb, no matter what.

"No, but they don't know what's going on."

"Why not?"

"Because I've been hiding the truth from them."

Her eyebrows flew above her hairline at that little morsel. "Are you admitting that you've been lying?"

"To them? Yes." He dropped his chin down. "To you? No."

But Amber had had enough. "Look, I'm sure you've woven together this complicated tapestry of cause and effect where somehow I owe you more than I've already given. But trust me, I don't, and I never will. So you can save yourself a bunch of trouble by getting out of here on your own recognizance. I'd rather not invoke my right to call on security."

He flinched so dramatically that the gesture could've been backlit with neon colors. "Don't call security, Amber. Please. You don't know what all's happened to me..."

"You're right," she said, not about to let him go on. "I don't. Nor do I need to know."

"If you'll just let me exp—"

"*You dumped me!*" she yelled, even though she hadn't intended to. "Not once but twice and for the tritest of reasons. Why should I let you explain anything ever?"

"Because I *need* you," he said, stressing his words.

"Well, I needed you too, as I recall. Perhaps you remember how all that turned out." Amber's breaths sawed in and out of her lungs as if she'd just climbed to the highest elevation on the Franklin Mountains.

"I'm sorry."

"No." She raised a hand palm out. "I'm sick of your apologies. I don't trust them, and I don't trust you."

He gusted out a quiet sigh, and it registered that he wasn't arguing back. She'd insulted him, had injected her voice with pure venom, and he had yet to volley any of the same her way. Whatever game he was attempting to initiate, she refused to play.

"Am…"

"Get out."

At that, his head jerked up and his gaze again met hers. Finally, he appeared to understand that she wasn't kidding. Only then did she pick up on something she hadn't till now. His features looked different. Not that he hadn't retained the attractiveness he'd always had, but his skin seemed sallower, his cheeks gaunt. His blue eyes appeared dull and lifeless. And his clothing appeared to be hanging on him differently, as if he'd exchanged them all for garments a size or two too big.

On an impulse, she reached inside of his jacket and through one sleeve to pinch his left bicep in her hand. The musculature that had always been there wasn't anymore. No wonder he'd gone where she'd led him. He was noticeably thinner. To the point of being underweight.

"Are you ill?" she asked him, transitioning automatically into physician mode. Maybe she wasn't over what he'd done to her, but her instinct was to care for the injured, infirm, or anyone in pain. Amber couldn't ignore her Hippocratic Oath or need to assist others. They were who she was as a person.

"No, I'm just… having a hard time of it." He paused as if expecting her to interrupt, only going on when she didn't. "Did you hear about the civil suit against me?"

She frowned. "No."

"Well, I was sued and lost a few months back. Since then, I've had to move out of my house and sell pretty much everything of value that I owned. It probably wouldn't be so bad if I could find work, but my reputation is so tarnished that no firms will hire me. I've been living in the Motel 6, but I'm almost out of the little cash I had. They're going to evict me soon. And maybe this sounds like some fabricated sob story to you, but I swear it's true. It's probably even a part of public record somewhere, at least the civil suit will be. I can't go to Mom or Mia because I told them I moved back to Cali."

"Wait," she said, stopping his narrative. "Why tell your family that you moved?"

"Because they know I was fired, but I told them I was hired with another firm. Then, I told them I was transferred out of state."

"I don't understand this weird compulsion of yours to—" Now he interrupted her.

"Lie to them. Yeah, I know. But you didn't grow up being told you were the man of the house at a really young age. They believe in me. They're counting on me to watch out for them and be someone important. A pillar of the community." Just when she felt like rolling her eyes at him, his tone became even more solemn than it had been. Not only that, there was a desperation in his eyes that she'd never seen. "I *can't* disappoint them. I *can't* let them down."

"What happens if you accidentally run into them somewhere?"

"I'll come up with a cover story. I'm fast on my feet. Or I used to be. Just… please help me one more time."

"Have you been eating?" she asked, and for some reason, that question reignited his pride. The haughty cockiness that she'd always seen within him made a reappearance.

"Sure."

"How often is that?"

He scowled at her, then averted his gaze again. "I'm using what's left in my bank account to pay for my current accommodations and a few groceries. When that's gone, I'll move into my car."

Keeping her arms crossed, she paced in front of him. While she hadn't imagined a scenario where she'd actually contemplate helping this man again, she couldn't let him trudge out of here knowing his next bed would be in his car, even if it was a gigantic Hummer.

"Is it your Hummer you'll be staying in?" At least then he'd have to space to spread out, though her conscience screamed at that idea.

"No," he muttered.

"Which one, then? The Maserati? The Corvette?" Neither of those was very spacious, so she hoped not.

"I sold all those."

"Then what car are you talking about?"

"I bought a Ford Taurus," he mumbled out. "It's a few years old."

She had to crane her neck toward him to hear his answer, he'd been so quiet in his delivery. There'd been more than once that she'd wished Troy Sykes would get knocked down a peg or two, and evidently, that exact thing had come to pass. She'd thought it'd make her feel better, but revenge didn't taste so good to her after all. All hearing this had done was make her pity him.

Still, she wouldn't be manipulated by him ever again. So she instigated a bit of an insurance policy.

"You broke your word to me, so now, I can't trust it," she told him, standing up straight.

"But…"

She didn't interrupt him this time; instead, she raised one hand in a stop motion. He fell silent. "So if I help you, I'll need to have some collateral. That way, if you attempt to deceive me or not keep good faith, I'll be compensated." She didn't give a single iota about compensation; all she wanted was for him to follow through on his promises, not that he needed to know that.

He visibly swallowed. "I don't have much in the way of belongings anymore."

"That's not what I mean. You haven't been disbarred, correct?"

"Of course not," he looked offended.

"Then in order for me to scratch your back, you'll scratch mine by taking whatever position I find for you."

Troy nodded vigorously. "Okay."

"Even if that position involves more hours and less pay? You'll make a living, though it'll be considerably less than you're accustomed to," she pointed out.

"Right now, I'm making nothing, so I don't have much room to disagree, do I?"

"You really don't."

"This'll be something attorney-based, right?"

"Right," she assured him, though it wouldn't be much like what he'd done in his past.

"Fine. I agree to do whatever you can get me."

Taking a deep breath, she dropped her arms and went to sit at her desk. She typed what she needed into the search engine. "Can you provide me with a résumé?"

"Um…" He scratched the back of his neck. "Yeah. I can do that."

"All right. Once you have one drawn up, send it over to my email."

"Is your email blocked from me like your phone and text messages are?"

Ooh, busted. "I'll change that. Just pop it over to me, and I'll go from there. There's always a shortage of this position, so your chances should be good."

"Are you going to tell me what I'm supposed to be doing?"

"If and when the job comes through, I'll let you know," she said, feeling more triumphant than was strictly necessary. Technically, she held Troy's future in her hands, and having that much power over a man who'd hurt her was somewhat heady. Not that she'd ever abuse that power, even if she was the teeniest bit tempted.

He quirked up one side of his mouth. "Guess I'm at your mercy." He twisted around and went out the way he'd come in, but the dullness she'd seen in his eyes had dissipated. And though she decided not to rub his nose in it more than she already had, he'd called the situation correctly.

Troy Sykes was most definitely at her mercy.

CHAPTER TWELVE

TROY SAT AT ONE OF THE COMPUTER STATIONS AT THE Richard Burges Branch of the local public library and logged into his saved documents on his OneDrive account. He couldn't deny that it felt disheartening to look through some of the file names present. He'd maintained a habit of keeping any documents he thought might require a backup and mulling over these now reminded him of the professional he still considered himself to be.

There were copies of important links to mostly Californian legal sites, as well as photos of himself and the other members of his firm there in Los Angeles, all wearing the knowing smiles of success. He paused on one particular image. Troy had been laughing, so whoever had taken this had caught him in an open-mouthed grin. He'd been standing straight and tall with a posture that spoke of poise and assurance. He didn't remember what had made him laugh like that, but what hit him was that he couldn't remember the last time he'd laughed *period*.

It would've had to have been before the Adams case, that was for sure.

He glared around at his current location. Most of the patrons were either students or elderly people who kept asking for the librarian's attention to help them find things on the internet. The last time he'd personally been in a library had been in his law school days. Even then, it'd never been so he could use a desktop computer touched by who knew how many kids' sticky hands. Before all this had happened to him, he'd had unlimited access to whatever he needed. He hadn't had to reserve a slot at a keyboard where both the C and D keys were missing.

The ironic thing was the Motel 6 did have Wi-Fi, but since he'd had to sell his laptop, the only access he had to it was through his phone. And now, he needed to refresh his résumé and download it to Amber's email. He pulled it up. The thing had been as slick as he could make it. Well, actually, he hadn't made it himself at all. Prior to receiving his first gig as an attorney in Cali, he'd hired another student to create one for him.

For a measly fifty bucks, the girl had taken his information and a pic of him in a suit and had put together what he'd considered a masterpiece. It had his professionally taken photo at the top and two sleek navy lines horizontally separating his personal info and pic from the rest. A matching set of lines then ran vertically along the left-hand side. His buddies had taken one look at it and proclaimed it to be "epically dope, bro." He'd agreed.

Back then, he'd felt like the king of the world. Now, not so much.

All his suits and everything else he owned with the exception of the suitcase he lived out of resided in the back seat and trunk of his Taurus. But if Amber could pull some strings and somehow pluck a lawyer position for him out of her magic hat, maybe he could start to rebuild what remained of his career.

Then, it occurred to him that Amber might be doing a number on him. What if this was all some elaborate prank? What if this was about some vengeance plot she had against him for breaking up with her? He might not have believed it of her before seeing her spit nails at him, but now, he had a different impression. Would she set him up just to watch him take a fall?

He honestly didn't know.

Regardless, he had to trust her. What alternative did he have?

So, Troy updated his résumé, saved it to the cloud, and sent it as an attachment to Amber's work and home email, just like she'd asked him to. Now, the results of whatever might happen were no longer in his hands.

A week went by with no word from Amber, and worry dogged him with every heartbeat. At this point, he had enough money to pay for two more nights of lodging and a single meal each day. He'd taken to eating at a Mexican place nearby because they offered inexpensive lunch platters that came with free salsa and chips, and he could fill up that way.

But he was about to come to the end of the road. He went to the local dollar store—an establishment he'd never set one foot in prior to now—and bought as much nonperishable food as he could. He hadn't been this close to starvation since he'd been a kid and his mom cooked potatoes over and over because that was all that they had available from their garden.

On the door was a "Now Hiring" sign, and at the checkout, he brought it up to the cashier.

"What positions are you hiring for? Manager? Assistant manager?"

"Cashier here at the registers," she told him. "Though just so you know, if there's no customers checking out, you'll also be stocking, cleaning, and whatever else the manager says."

"How much does cashiering pay?"

"Minimum wage."

The idea of spending all that time, money, and effort to complete his law degree only to go to work at the local dollar store for minimum wage frankly made him sick to his stomach. Would working minimum wage even be enough to keep him off the streets?

"How many hours would that position receive?" he asked her next.

"Part time, so it fluctuates. Right now, I'm getting more 'cause we're shorthanded, but other times it'll be around twenty-five hours a week or so."

He did a quick tally in his head. If all he received were twenty-five hours a week, his paycheck would cover only three or four days of lodgings before his account went dry. No minimum wage position would be enough unless he had two or more of them. Someone from the back of their extremely long line spoke up.

"What's taking so long?"

"Yeah, I don't got all day," someone else put in, so Troy paid.

"You wanna application?"

Disheartened, he shook his head no. He carried his bags to his car, then found himself back inside his motel room with no memory of how he'd arrived there. Turning on the outdated television just so he wouldn't feel alone, he did his best to lose himself in an old sci-fi movie. Thinking about his life would be counterproductive, and he needed some sleep. Later, in the middle of the night, he jerked awake. He glanced up at the TV, wondering if the infomercial about some new vacuum system had woken him, when he heard a distinct bang on his door.

"I got the stuff. Let me in!" a man yelled, jangling hard on the handle. Troy's heart climbed up his throat as if to escape his body. He didn't recognize the voice.

"Lenny, man, open up!" The man continued to rattle the door in its frame as he let loose a stream of profanity.

As a jock surrounded constantly by buddies, beautiful girls, and hangers-on, Troy had rarely felt fearful or even nervous. Even as a defense attorney representing clients he knew for a fact were dangerous criminals, he'd never felt afraid to stand up for them in court. Now, though, Troy felt spikes of terror racing over his skin like the stings of fire ants.

After a few more minutes of this, followed by what sounded like the dude's fist on Troy's window, he heard the sound of door hinges squeaking somewhere down the way. There was a hushed reprimand, more curses from the same voice, then quiet. Pulse sprinting and lungs working overtime, it took Troy a long while to calm down.

Thinking maybe a hot shower would help, he lumbered over to the tiny bathroom. Twisting on the nozzle, he heard a collection of mini expulsions of air coming through the pipes instead of water. The faucet shot out a handful of rust-colored liquid, and then, there was nothing. Frustrated and annoyed, he pelted out of his bathroom to the motel's landline phone.

"Hey," he snapped once the front desk person answered. "My water isn't working."

There was an audible sigh. "Which room, sir?" the attendant said in a bored tone.

"112."

"I'll put in a maintenance ticket."

"When will it be fixed?"

"No way of knowing." Troy heard electronic beeping. Was this kid playing a handheld video game while on the phone with him?

"So you're saying that I'll have no way of showering for who knows how long?" Troy's voice cracked like a whip, and finally, that seemed to get the kid's attention.

"We have one last room available, sir. But it's upstairs."

"Does the water work in there?"

"It should," the kid said, but he sounded as if he had no idea. Perfect.

"What's the room number?"

"Uh... 222."

"Then get me access to that room. I'll be at the office in five minutes." He slammed down the headset.

Twenty minutes later, he'd transferred to room 222 and stepped into the bathroom stall, delighting in the hot running water. Said water ran out halfway through his shower, but at least he was able to get clean again. In his fresh T-shirt and pajama pants, Troy settled into his bed. A spring stuck into his spine as he did, and he shifted away from it. It was four in the morning, and he should've felt tired after the evening's ordeal. Instead, he felt restless.

He flipped on his television again to distract himself, but it only stayed on for about five seconds before blinking off again. He tried the remote several more times, all with the same results. He didn't know whether to roar in frustration, cackle like some comic book villain, or punch his fist through the thin wall.

A loud knock echoed through his room, ripping Troy from his slumber. He'd only dropped off to sleep sometime after dawn.

"Housekeeping..." came a woman's voice.

"Uh, I'm still in here. Do not disturb," he hollered out, feeling disoriented.

What time was it, anyway? He glanced at the alarm clock to see that it was nearly noon, which was the checkout

APRIL MURDOCK

time. He heard the metal cart roll away and rubbed his gritty eyes. Tonight would be his last night here, and then, he'd be in his car twenty-four seven. No bed. No running water. No legal place to park the thing. What would he do if he received a ticket or if the Taurus was towed? Where would he stay then?

He lay there on his side, his thoughts going down these increasingly dark corridors, when his phone chimed.

Amber: Found a job for you.

Troy grabbed at it so anxiously, his hands trembled.

"Where is it?" he asked her by way of greeting. "I'm still going to be an attorney, right?"

"Hello to you too," she quipped, then paused. "You feeling okay? You sound funny."

"I-I'm fine," he stammered, not supporting his case one bit.

"You still have a suit?"

"Yeah."

"Put it on and go to the county courthouse. Ask for Dennis Yang. He'll get you started."

CHAPTER THIRTEEN

AMBER MONITORED HER PATIENT'S BLOOD PRESSURE CAREFULLY as she lay on the free clinic's exam table. The lady didn't speak a word of English, so their communication back and forth had to be largely nonverbal. She laid a palm on the woman's distended abdomen and nodded, and the lady's brown eyes softened. Amber only knew a few words of Spanish, but thankfully those words proved helpful.

"*Descansas,*" she said, telling her patient to rest. The woman was in false labor, but her blood pressure skirted borderline high readings. She'd keep her for an hour or so to make certain she was in the safe zone before sending her home.

Her mind wandered to some of the research she'd done for Troy over this past week. Earlier that very afternoon over her lunch, she'd driven by the Motel 6 where he'd been staying and regarded his current form of transportation. If she hadn't seen him get into the rusted-out bucket of bolts with her own eyes, she might not have believed the car to be his.

APRIL MURDOCK

In all the years she'd known him, he'd always had the best and flashiest of everything. He'd prided himself on it. Yet, there he was, in one of his expensive high-end suits—which he kept running his hands over to flatten out the odd wrinkle or two—ducking down to get into a car he once would've referred to as a "heap."

Oh, how the mighty had fallen.

Yet, while she might've felt a brief spate of satisfaction at how things were going for him early on, she hadn't been able to hold on to that feeling for long without censuring herself. The man had been humbled to such a strong degree that he barely resembled himself, and feeling good about that felt wrong to her.

She remembered one of the deliveries she'd had when still a resident. The woman had suffered a lot of issues during her third trimester, including gestational diabetes. Her baby grew to be dangerously large for a woman her size, and when she went to give birth, both she and her baby had nearly died. Amber recalled her attending barking orders at her, and Amber had done her best to follow them. In the end, both mother and child survived, and Amber had left the OR to go track down the husband they'd kicked out an hour earlier because he'd been in the way.

She'd found him leaning against one wall opposite the waiting room all by himself. He hadn't been given the chance to put on the required scrubs over his clothing, so he'd been in a suit and tie much like the kind Troy wore, showing that he'd come straight from his job. Then, as she approached, she heard the choked sounds of weeping.

"Mr. Bailey?" she'd murmured in order not to startle him. As he twisted around, she'd placed a hand on his shoulder. "Mr. Bailey, your wife and son are okay."

His head had bolted up so fast that she'd been tempted to take a step back.

"Donna didn't die?" he asked, his voice a mess.

"No."

"And… and the baby?"

"He's fine," Amber reiterated. "He weighs fourteen pounds, thirteen ounces, which is why Dr. Hudson had to do an emergency caesarian, but he's fine. They're both fine and resting."

But the man's tears kept coming. "I've been neglecting her to get this promotion at work. And I thought… I thought…"

Amber knew what he'd thought and understood that the best remedy would be to bring him to his wife's room and introduce him to his infant son. He and his wife had wept even harder then, but the quality of that weeping had transformed into relief and joy.

It'd been the most moving sight she'd ever witnessed and a reminder to not take things for granted. Life was too short for that.

Not that she had any delusions about Troy ever learning such a lesson. The man might have a first-rate intellect, but emotionally, he was incapable of such an insight. Yet she didn't want even someone like him to be brought to his knees or found dead in a gutter somewhere. Maybe on the day he'd broken up with her last time she wouldn't have minded giving in to her basest impulses, but now Amber wanted to rise above that.

She thought of Gandhi's quote, "An eye for an eye only makes the whole world blind."

What would be the sense in that?

Since all she had today was a single morning shift at the clinic, she drove to a neighborhood tucked between the UTEP campus and the courthouse later that afternoon. There on a quiet street was a huge old Victorian that had been converted into affordable one-bedroom apartments. The area wasn't fancy, but the crime rates stayed low. Also, the place had been well cared for and kept clean. For her purposes, it would do.

Amber hadn't received any texts or calls from Troy yet, but considering that no phones were allowed in the court-house, the mystery ended there. Curious as to how his first foray into this unknown realm had gone, she waited until all the courts were in adjournment for the day, then called him. It rang four times, then went to voicemail, telling her he hadn't freed himself yet. But then, as she was about to record a message for him to call her back, he picked up.

"You made me a public defender?" he demanded without preamble, sounding incredulous, and Amber felt torn between an amused snicker and exasperation. She decided to answer in kind.

"Oh, you're welcome. It was no trouble at all to track down my third cousin who's a court recorder in Dallas and ask her what I needed to do to secure you a steady job as a lawyer again." Silence filled the line between them, so she pushed forward again. "And, by the way, you're also welcome for the new place of residence you now have that's located five blocks away from the courthouse. I'm sure you're exceedingly grateful to me, the ex-girlfriend who didn't have to lift a finger to help you but did."

Whoa. She hadn't meant to give him both barrels like that, but what'd been said was already out there in the ether.

"You found me another place to live?" he asked, his voice faint.

"Yes. It's nothing like your former palatial mansion. It's a one-bedroom, one-bath that's nothing special, but it's better than a Motel 6 or your car. Since public defending is a state job, you'll only get paid monthly, so I took care of the first couple months of rent for you until you're back on your feet." When he said nothing, she pressed on. "This is where you say, 'thank you,' Troy."

"Thank you," he parroted back at her. Eh, it was better than nothing, even if she'd had to prompt him.

She disconnected the line and took a deep breath. She blew it out slowly like a yoga teacher might instruct her to do, releasing all the negativity dealing with Troy Sykes had saturated her with. It felt like closing a bad chapter in her life and turning the page to start over with a fresh slate. She wished him well, then headed to her dad's favorite burger joint. She contacted him through the app on her car's radio.

"Hey, Daddy, it's me. Have you eaten dinner yet?"

"Nope, precious. I'm just now pulling into my driveway."

"Awesome. I'll be there shortly."

They'd sat in her dad's backyard, enjoying the unseasonably mild February evening. It wasn't unheard of for the temperatures in El Paso to float right up to the sixties or even seventies during this time of year, though typically, such weather didn't last long.

"You know what the best part of a warm day in winter is?" she asked him, peering out at the Franklin Mountains, which, despite the heat of the day, had peaks still dusted with white.

"What?"

"No bugs."

He chuckled. "Would've been a good day for a hike."

"Yep," she said, remembering how frequently she and her dad had ventured up there when she'd been a kid. Her memories shimmered bright and beautiful at the forefront of her mind. She sniffled unexpectedly, her eyes burning.

Her dad sat up and put a hand on her knee. "What is it, Amber?"

"Nothing," she said, but the clogged sound of her voice betrayed her. "I don't know. You were such a great dad, and I had a wonderful childhood. I guess maybe I'm feeling maudlin for no reason."

It wasn't for no reason, but she couldn't tell her dad that. She couldn't admit that while she felt ecstatic that he'd found someone, she doubted she'd ever find that for herself.

"Precious, thirty really isn't that old, you know," her dad said.

Thirty. She would be turning the big three-oh on her next birthday, even though it remained a few months away. Theoretically, she knew thirty wasn't old, but somewhere within the recesses of her soul, a clock had started ticking. And she fretted about what it might be counting down to.

"I know. It's just that life seems to be speeding up. When I was young it used to drag by, but now…"

"I hate to say it, but don't plan on that changing any time soon. In fact, the older you get, the faster it goes."

That was what she was afraid of.

CHAPTER FOURTEEN

BEING A PUBLIC DEFENDER RESEMBLED BEING A DEFENSE lawyer about as much as a stagehand resembled the lead star in a play. They were both a part of the production, but one person's job was far more menial than the other's. From the second Troy traipsed into that courthouse till the moment he left it, he seldom had time to so much as catch his breath. He went from one lowlife—he supposed he should refer to them as *clients*—to the next, interrogating them as rapidly as a gameshow host, then thrusting them before the judge.

It was like speed dating for arrested people.

Not once had he felt prepared enough to present a relevant case for them, but that didn't matter. The assembly line just kept bearing down on him. He had to stand up for people who were often wearing clothing deemed inappropriate for *any* formal meeting, much less a trial. A few times, his clients had been taken in nothing but sleepwear. These folks had to be given prison jumpsuits. And it was in that state—already looking like criminals—that they would be placed in front of someone who would determine whether to set them free or convict them.

This upped the difficulty level of Troy's job by about a thousand.

He'd only been doing this for one week, and he'd already defended against every lower-level crime known to man. He never would've associated with any of these people in either his personal life or as a defense attorney. These were the dregs of society. His first day, he'd felt so creeped out by being their counsel that he'd had to force himself not to cringe away.

This certainly hadn't been what he'd pictured as he'd aced all of his classes back in law school.

While he had yet to see Amber as a visitor in any of his court proceedings, he wondered if secretly, she was laughing her head off at his discomfort. All this felt far too similar to his own time behind bars, and he really and truly detested the reminder.

One thing he couldn't detest was his new apartment. The place might be small and have only the most minimal of furnishings and appliances, but it was much better than either the Motel 6 or his car. Every time he walked into it, he felt relieved to have his own space again. So far, knowing he had a real residence to return to was the only thing keeping him going.

He kept anticipating a call or text from Amber, but none had come. Would she simply pop by to check up on him? He glanced outside his second-story bedroom window to watch the two palm trees swaying gently out next to the street. This neighborhood might not have much on his old one, but other than the occasional siren from a passing ambulance or firetruck, it was delightfully peaceful.

He sighed. He supposed having somewhere to hang his metaphorical hat made what he was struggling with at work worth it.

Since he no longer had to drain his meager savings on payments to the Motel 6, he spent some of it on better groceries. Orange juice. Bread, lettuce, tomatoes, and lunch meat. Canned soup. A couple of microwavable meals. A deep-dish pizza from the freezer section. That Saturday at noon, he pulled that pizza out to cook it for lunch.

Something about seeing the pizza on his stovetop brought back the memory of when he had ordered in a couple of supremes for him and Amber to share. But instead of remembering the aroma of the pizza toppings, he thought of her scent before dinner had arrived. What had her individual fragrance been? It had always made him think of nurseries full of infants...

Infants. That was it. Amber smelled like *baby lotion*.

How else would a woman surrounded by babies smell? And how had he gone so long without thinking about that? Man, he missed her.

Back at UTEP, he and Amber had been together all the time. She might not have been his first kiss, but she'd been his first real girlfriend. They'd studied together, gone out on dates every weekend, and she'd shown up to every single one of his baseball games to cheer him on.

He could recall glancing up into the stands right behind the dugout and finding her there, the little pixie girl with the big smile. When they'd trekked across campus, they'd meander hand in hand, her diminutive palm soft against his. She'd always seemed so excited to see him, and it'd made him feel like some kind of superhero.

Then, earlier this year when they'd gone out again, she'd willingly carved time out of her busy schedule to be with him. Originally, he'd taken her to gatherings held by his partners, displaying her gorgeousness like a trophy. But after that, they'd become much more casual with each other, hanging out at his place in front of his big-screen TV.

Having her around had felt... homey, somehow. Like when he'd been little and his mom had carried him in her arms. It didn't make much sense now that he thought about it, but that was why he kept returning to Amber over and over again. It wasn't just that she was beautiful, though she absolutely was. Having Amber nearby felt right. Also, he knew no matter what, he could count on her. Rely on her.

Even when he hadn't returned the favor.

A pain stabbed into his diaphragm then, the sensation taking him by surprise. Amber had come through for him this time too. When he felt like he couldn't go to anyone else, he'd reached out to her. And although they were no longer a couple, she'd gone out of her way to help him. Somehow, he'd known that she would. Because she was just that good of a person. He'd believed she wouldn't let him down, and she hadn't.

Not once.

He peered around at his living space. Wouldn't it be nice if she were here with him right now? Over the past few months, his life had imploded in spectacular fashion, and he'd been on his own to cope. Or had he? There'd been one person he could trust who'd stayed by his side, at least metaphorically. And that person had been Amber.

That person had always been Amber.

Since hitting adulthood, and especially since attaining his law degree, he felt like he'd needed to be this icon of strength and power when it came to his family. His mother could only see him as her golden boy, her devoted son, the man of the house. And he'd wanted his baby sister, Mia, to think of him as invulnerable. Unstoppable. Someone she could go to anytime she needed him.

Brett was his best bud, his comrade in arms, his colleague, and even his brother-in-law in both spirit and deed. Yet when Troy's career had jumped off the proverbial cliff, he hadn't felt like he could go to him. He hadn't felt like he could go to any of his family members. He hadn't wanted them to know. He'd needed to maintain that image of superiority and indestructibility where the three of them were concerned.

So, he'd dialed up Amber and confided in her instead. He'd reestablished contact even after breaking up with her. She'd been mad at him, telling him off. And for some reason, that memory made another he'd thought long buried rise to the surface. His mother thundering at his father. Troy shut his eyes. He didn't want to remember, but his automatic recall brought it to the forefront of his mind anyway.

"You can't leave us like this," his mom had insisted, chasing after his father with a newborn Mia over one shoulder.

Mia had been fussy despite his mother's cradling of her, and Troy—still a little boy in kindergarten—had been cowering in the next room, observing their argument through an opening in the curtains. He didn't want his daddy to leave, but his parents' snarling voices had frightened him.

"Get away from me."

"Brooks," his mother's shouting had taken on a note of pleading. "I need you. Your children need you."

"I don't care."

He didn't care. Those words had imprinted on Troy's youthful brain like some hideous tattoo. His mom and dad's fight ended when a door banged shut. There'd been silence, then crying. His mother's. Mia's.

His own.

And from out of nowhere, a voice hissed at the back of Troy's conscience, "You disrespected Amber in the same way, and the second time you strung her along like a cat tormenting a mouse. Which makes you not just as bad as your father, it makes you even *worse*."

At that thought, something happened inside Troy. This schism appeared, separating the opposing parts of himself like a Biblical earthquake tearing two continents asunder. It was as if his identity fractured, allowing the compartmentalized pieces he'd kept purposely apart to smush together. The arrogant pieces mixed with his doubts. His successes became overshadowed by his recent failures. And the realization of what he'd just discovered about himself shattered his preconceptions about who he'd been.

He'd always thought he was a good person deep down, but his actions hadn't borne that out, as his own perfect recall could attest. If anything, his actions proved that the inverse was true. He remembered what he'd said to Amber during their last split. The split that he'd caused. He saw the words emblazoned behind his eyes like they'd been written there in permanent ink.

I think we need to call it quits.

I don't have time for a girlfriend.

I'm just too preoccupied.

I'll hit you up afterwards maybe.

I can't make any promises.

He'd said all that to Amber. Behaved as if she'd basically been a stranger he'd crossed paths with instead of someone who meant the world to him. Someone who'd changed his life for the better every time she'd entered it. Why hadn't he absorbed what he'd done until now? Why hadn't he comprehended just how much he'd lost when he'd carelessly brushed her aside?

Like his father had cast his sister, his mom, and him aside.

He loathed his father. Loathed the man who'd ignored his mother's cries as well as his and stormed out of their house never to return. How could he hate his father as much as he did and yet morph into someone even worse than he was?

After collapsing on his bed, he noticed the room had started to shake. Had that earthquake he'd imagined been real? But no. Eventually he understood it wasn't the room shaking but him. He lay there trembling from head to foot as torment and guilt rose within him like a tide. It crashed over the top of him until it took him down to rock bottom, seizing him like an undertow and keeping him under until he couldn't breathe.

Until he'd been drowned for good.

CHAPTER FIFTEEN

Sipping her first swig of coffee, Amber prepared to familiarize herself with every patient on her ward. Luckily, at that instant there were only four: a mother who'd already delivered and would likely be released within a couple of hours, a woman in her first trimester who needed a checkup, another in her second, and a last one who was overdue.

If the fourth one didn't go into labor in the next few days, she'd have to induce, which she hesitated to do. She had to evaluate which would cause more harm—the Pitocin they'd have to flood her system with or the misery carrying a forty-two-week fetus would cost her. Hopefully, nature would take its course and the decision would be taken out of her hands.

Amber had been standing by one of the nurses' stations so she could finish her coffee uninterrupted when the phone rang, and one of the nurses answered.

"Le Mesa Medical Center Birthing Ward." Seconds passed as she listened, then curiously enough, she glanced up at Amber. "Hold, please." To her she said, "Dr. Crawford, you have a call. Apparently, they already dialed your cell and left a message, but they're saying it's a matter of some urgency."

"Which patient?" she asked, mentally listing the mothers and mothers-to-be in her head who were nearing their due dates.

"It's not a patient. It's the El Paso County Courthouse. They're asking about a Troy—"

"Sykes," Amber finished for her, irritation shortening her tone. What had he done now? "I'll take it." She picked up the hospital's landline. By the time she hung up, she was seething. In fact, she wouldn't have been too shocked to discover steam fuming from her ears. She marched over to Grace's office with red tinging her vision. She hoped she didn't have an aneurysm today. It would be highly inconvenient. "Gracie, I know I have awful timing, but I have to go."

Grace's face whitened. "Is it your dad?"

"Oh no. It's…" she trailed off. *Snow cones.* While she'd told her best friend all about her breakups with Troy—both of them—as well as her springing him from the slammer, she'd neglected to inform her about her latest round of assistance. She'd felt like Grace wouldn't approve, and she didn't feel like hearing a lecture. "It's something else. I do need to go, though. I'm so sorry to leave you in a lurch."

"No worries. Do whatever you need to. You know I've got your back."

Yes, she did. Thank goodness she had her bestie for a colleague. She honestly didn't know what she'd do without her. "You're the best, really," she said, yet for some reason, that specific sentiment felt wrong. She didn't recognize where it came from until she'd reached her Audi, then it dawned on her.

Troy had been the one to use that as a clichéd farewell. He'd even said it when he'd broken up with her.

Ugh!

The man had somehow embedded himself in her psyche against her will. And considering what he'd just done—or not done—she could throttle him with her bare hands. Every time she thought she'd rinsed her hands of him, he showed up again like a bad penny. She was going to have to take a firm stand and tell him she was through. Her ex was a user, plain and simple. He would take and take and take until she had nothing to give and not even worry about doing it.

But everyone had their limit, and she'd reached hers. Amber considered herself a patient woman, but enough was enough, for heaven's sake. It was past time she drew her line in the sand and forbade him from crossing it.

She drove over to the apartment she'd rented in his name as speedily as she safely could. Amber craved to get this over with ASAP. Once she arrived, she pounded on his door like a boxing champ.

"Troy Edward Sykes, you open up right now!" she bellowed out, fed up so completely, she'd middle-named him. "How could you flake on this job? Not showing up or calling in? That's juvenile behavior, not what's expected of a grown man like you. Do you hear me?"

She was making a spectacle of herself, she knew, but she didn't care. Amber felt so livid that every muscle in her body was as tight as a drawn bow. Jangling the doorknob, she found it locked. "By the way, I have my own key, and if you don't pull this door open by the time I count to ten, I'm unlocking it myself. One, two, three…"

Amber counted, her volume higher and higher with each number. By the time she reached ten, she was fit to be tied. "Fine. I'm coming in," she warned, and twisting her key, clicked the deadbolt and the small lock built into the knob.

His residence appeared dark as if no one was home, but then she heard a muted sound coming from the bedroom. A new notion flew into her brain, the possibility that he might be injured or in trouble somehow. To her knowledge, the man hadn't been one to play hooky from work before. What if something was wrong?

"Troy, I'm coming into your room," she called out again, padding along much more cautiously now.

What if someone had broken in here and attacked him? But no, the door had been locked from within. Her mind spun, thinking up possibilities for his absence and discarding them just as quickly. His bedroom door stood ajar. She caught sight of the lump on his bed and approached, finding him on his right side on his mattress. He lay above the covers in his pajamas, but he'd wrapped the comforter around him from below as if freezing.

Her first impression was that he was unconscious, but when she checked him more closely, she found his eyes open. He appeared to be awake but nonresponsive. Trans-ferring immediately into doctor mode, she leaned down next to him.

It remained too dark to see him clearly, and she peeked up, deciding the curtains were closer than the light switch. Casting them to the sides of his window frame, Amber rushed back to him, now noticing that the skin around his lips looked whiter than usual, almost bluish. The rest of his complexion had an unnatural pallor and clamminess to it as well, setting off warnings in her brain.

Using the flashlight on her phone, she studied his pupils and touched his forehead. He wasn't feverish and his pupils weren't dilated, but he presented the symptoms of a victim in shock. She took one of his hands, then the other, finding them cold. Too cold. To run down any obvious possibilities, she started asking him questions as she exam-ined him further.

"Troy, are you all right? Can you say anything? Do you know who I am?"

Nothing.

"Have you taken something?" Amber jerked her head around and searched for any evidence of an overdose. A syringe. A bottle of pills. Anything. She saw no such evidence, but relief didn't come. "Are you unwell? Did you fall and hit your head? Did something else happen?"

He remained catatonic.

She checked his pulse, which felt a bit too rapid, but his airways sounded clear. He continued to stare unfocused into space, not speaking or responding to stimuli. His skull rested on the sheets he'd exposed, so she rolled him onto his back and elevated his feet with both of his bed pillows. Going to the narrow closet, she found a blanket and covered him with it, then went to the thermostat and cranked it up to eighty.

A blare of static made her jump, but it wasn't coming from within his apartment. The static cleared to become a discernible radio report she could hear every word of. She listened, which wasn't hard; the walls in this complex must be paper thin. It wasn't a radio report after all. From the content, it had to be a police scanner. But that didn't matter right now.

She returned to his side and sat next to him on the bed, deciding that she probably needed to call an ambulance. Since he was literally a foot taller than her and outweighed her by at least a hundred pounds, she couldn't hope to drag him out to her vehicle on her own. Only once she'd opened her phone app did she hear a weak voice.

"Am?"

It was Troy, but it didn't sound anything like him. She leaned in close again, analyzing his features for any outward signs of pain or distress.

"I'm here," she told him. "Right here. Can you tell me what's wrong?"

"I…" He shook his head slightly, then nodded, but didn't elaborate. Clearly, he remained in a state of confusion. She went down her list of questions again.

"Have you taken anything? Any prescription medications or over-the-counter stuff?"

He paused, then shook his head again.

"Are you sick or have you fallen?"

Another shake.

Just to be thorough, she pressed the back of her hand to his cheek, checking his temperature once more. Moving lightning fast, he grabbed it, bringing her hand to his mouth.

He kissed the inside of her palm, then proceeded to murmur in the most heartfelt tone she'd ever heard from him, "I'm sorry. I'm so, so sorry."

Before she could pull away, he sat up, bracketing one of his arms around her back as he yanked her body in closer to his. She pondered whether he was aware of what he was doing or if he intended that apology for her. Maybe he'd had some sort of break with reality. If so, he could be dangerous. She was about to try to separate herself from him again when he gasped.

Fearful that his breathing had suddenly become compromised in some way, she pressed a hand to the back of his ribcage. But rather than sounding like he couldn't catch his breath, his chest hitched as if experiencing a hiccup. In fact, his whole body jerked. And right after that, the man burst into sobs.

Amber held herself motionless, staggered by this realization.

She'd sped over here ready to chew him up one side and down the other for blowing off his public defender responsibilities, only to find this. Still uncertain of the overall state of his health, she remained in his embrace, patting his left shoulder blade awkwardly. The sobbing only escalated

APRIL MURDOCK

at that point, the broken timbre of his deep voice reverberating against the walls of his bedroom. It was as if his feelings could no longer be contained, so she made soothing noises, hoping to calm him.

His reaction seemed so extreme that she dropped her phone and rubbed up and down his spine, feeling for any injuries or other issues that might need to be treated. She found nothing conclusive as he cried harder and harder, almost like a child who'd had some sort of severe upset or trauma. Tears dampened her coat and the neck of her scrubs shirt, and she began to grow more concerned. It was clear that he needed to get out whatever this was, but she still couldn't determine if this had been brought on by some sort of medical condition.

Even as the physician in her thought this, though, she realized that she'd never once witnessed this level of emotion from Troy. Nothing even close to this. He was being wracked by sobs so fierce, they were literally shuddering through both of them. Needing to do more, she repositioned herself so she could hold him more securely and rock him back and forth. Watching this outpouring of... whatever this was, baffled her. Where was all this coming from?

Thinking that maybe him talking about it would help, she pried a bit further.

"Troy, has something happened to someone you care about? Are your mom and little sister okay?"

This query finally tugged him back into a more stable state. Like an engine winding down, the noises he'd been making slowed, then gradually came to a halt. He kept his face buried in her neck, continuing to hug her as if his life depended on it. Not that she could push him away. Busting up their connection right now would feel downright mean.

"No, but I..." He gulped down air as if suffocating. Maybe he was. "I didn't want this."

"Didn't want what?" she asked him, eager to get to the bottom of his outburst.

He raised both hands to wipe at his cheeks, and she stood, hustling to his bathroom and back to provide him with some tissues to mop himself up with. He peeked up briefly, showing her just how badly his features had been wrecked. His eyes were bloodshot and remained tear-filled, and his complexion looked almost as red and puffy as someone who'd been repeatedly punched in the face.

In the midst of cleaning up, he muttered an ambiguous, "Didn't want to be anything like him."

"Like who?"

"Brooks."

Instead of sitting on the bed again, Amber knelt on one knee, her petite stature meaning she remained at his eye level. She'd heard that name somewhere and took a reasonable guess. "Is Brooks your dad?"

He nodded, the motion jerky and somehow bitter. "But I don't think of that man as my dad. He left Mom and the two of us kids with nothing so he could go off with some other woman. And he hasn't tried to reach out to any of us since. No calls. No texts. No emails. Not even a letter. He discarded us. His own family. But..." More tears cascaded down his cheeks as he looked away from her. "As repre-hensible as he is, I'm worse."

She couldn't seem to grasp precisely what Troy's father had to do with his breakdown.

"Why do you think you're worse?"

"Because of how I've been living…" There was a long pause as he brushed at his eyes then peered wearily out his window. "But mostly because of what I did to you." She followed his gaze, spotting the fronds of two palm trees being tossed around by the chilly February wind. "I returned all your sweetness and devotion with nothing but selfish disregard. I don't know why you keep putting up with me. I don't even understand why you're here now."

"Maybe I'm vying for sainthood," she suggested wryly, going for some lightness. She didn't want to mention the courthouse or the duties he'd shirked, especially since he'd had legitimate reasons for doing so.

He gusted out an exhale and flicked his face in her direction before glancing away again. "You're already a saint in my book."

Amber brought her hand up to her barbell piercing, twisting it in place out of a sense of fretfulness. This was such uncharted territory. She'd never imagined coming over here to find a Troy Sykes totally overcome by sorrow and regret. It felt surreal.

It also occurred to her that he'd been in a bad state for a while. He might even have been teetering on the cusp of dehydration, so she backed away in order to go to his kitchen. Finding some cans of chicken noodle soup, she heated up some, then filled a tall glass with ice water. Not having a tray, she brought him first the water, ordering him to drink. Then she returned with the soup, having poured it into a deep ceramic bowl with an attached handle.

"Eat that. Every bite," she told him, and his light blue eyes —looking all the more vivid because of their red rims— latched onto hers.

"You'd make a great mom. You're so caring, you know." Then, he applied himself to doing what she'd said.

Amber gaped at him. She'd been praised as a physician, but no one had ever suggested that those skills might apply to her as a future mother. It was one of the kindest, most astonishing things anyone had ever said to her, and it'd come from Troy of all people.

And if she were honest, she didn't have a clue how to take it.

CHAPTER SIXTEEN

"I TRULY AM SORRY FOR HOW I BROKE UP WITH YOU. I KNOW I apologized before but..." It made Troy feel even more terrible to realize just how insincere he'd been with her in the past. "But I didn't mean it. Not then. I do, now, though. I swear to God that I do. I also know better than to expect your forgiveness. I don't deserve it, and I never will."

Maybe it was pointless of him to admit all this stuff to her. Maybe it wouldn't make any difference in her life at all, but he hoped it would. He hoped it helped her because losing control in front of Amber like this had been excruciating to him. Not to mention humiliating. He'd never been a crier, not even as a kid. Yet he'd cried so long and so hard a few minutes ago that he currently had the mother of all headaches.

Could be all this was his penance for hurting Amber. She was so much better than him. What was the woman even doing here? When he added up all the various methods of assistance she'd provided for him after he'd taken her heart and trampled it like some Texan mustang, it made him want to sock himself in the gut.

He wished he could make it up to her, but how? He was in no position whatsoever to offer her anything. Not a good reputation. Not a clear record. Not riches or a home. Not even the bare minimum of a happy history together. For some unconscionable reason, she kept providing him with generosity he hadn't earned while he'd dug himself deeper and deeper into her debt, financially and in every other way. He owed her so much now, it might be years before he could put a dent in it. Maybe even decades.

It wasn't exactly an enviable circumstance to be in.

She went to sit on his window ledge a couple of feet away, her tiny frame small enough she didn't even have to balance herself to do it. If he'd tried that, he would've gone splat on the floor. She reminded him of a lovely bird, her purple scrubs brightening the atmosphere of his room. He scrutinized her features as she situated herself there, taking in the long length of her lashes as they fluttered over her cheekbones.

Then, when they made eye contact, he catalogued the selection of colors in her hazel orbs. Around the outside rim, her iris was a deep navy blue. Inside of that was a pretty blue-green color, and around the pupil was a milk chocolate brown. Her eyes were mesmerizing, yet he hadn't bothered to notice that until now.

"I believe you," she answered him, simply. But then she sighed.

"It just doesn't fix anything," he concluded.

"No, I guess it doesn't. But I will say this. Someone like your father never would've done what you just did."

"What?" Bawl his eyes out?

"Face his mistakes like a man. That takes some real intestinal fortitude. Trust me, I know. I'm a doctor."

He snorted despite himself, feeling microscopically better. "I don't know how you can joke with me."

"Expressions of amusement and laughter come highly recommended. Since it softens life's rougher edges, I prescribe indulging in them as often as possible. Also, I happen to know that you have a quirky sense of humor." She sent him a half-smile that was so kind, the lump in his throat came back again. "The reason I'm here is because the courthouse contacted me about your absence."

Disoriented, he looked at his watch. It was late morning on a Monday. How had he missed that?

"You had a challenging weekend, I take it," Amber said, echoing his thoughts.

He dug his fingers into the nape of his neck. It'd been Saturday when he'd, well… lost his mind didn't even cover it. Troy still wasn't certain he could fully understand what he'd experienced. "Yeah, I did."

"How about I provide you with a doctor's excuse for today, and you start fresh tomorrow. Sound like a plan?"

"Yeah. Thank you, Am. I appreciate it." He stared straight into her hazel eyes as he expressed his gratitude.

She shifted off the windowsill and patted his arm. "I know you do."

After she left, he rinsed his face in cold water, then threw on some sweats and a jacket and went on a walk. Soon, moving so slowly got on his nerves so he accelerated into a jog. He found himself loping towards the courthouse and adjusted his trajectory to avoid being seen by someone who might report that he wasn't sick after all. As he did, he watched from a distance as a patrol car pulled up with someone in handcuffs.

In the past, he would've had one of two reactions to such a sight. On the extremely rare occasion that that person would've been his client, he would've stood at his client's side as his legal representative. Much more often, though, he would've looked down on whoever they were, assuming the worst about them. It wouldn't have been about thinking that person to be guilty as much as him not wanting to waste his time on someone who couldn't afford him.

Yet, he'd been that person himself. He'd been arrested and hauled into the system wearing handcuffs. He'd gone before a judge as a prisoner rather than a lawyer and failed to come out of the situation on the winning side. That person had once been him, and for the first time ever, he realized he could relate to their situations. Even while serving as a public defender last week, he'd noticed that each case—while usually small in scale—was unique.

Some of the people whom he represented had been arrested because they'd been at the wrong place at the wrong time. They were innocent. Some were guilty, but what they'd done had been a mistake. Some were guilty yet remained utterly unrepentant. Many, whether guilty or innocent, had shown fear or even terror when they'd faced the court. A handful had openly wept and/or begged for mercy. Troy had been repulsed by these clients, by what he'd always perceived as a weakness. But he didn't feel repulsed anymore.

Now that the shoe was on the other foot, he saw those same scenes with a fresh perspective that knocked him from his foundations.

Everyone deserved representation, someone to be on their side and listen to them. So, the next morning when he went back to work, he saw each client differently. His first client was dirty, as in wearing clothing and shoes that had literal dirt stains. He didn't see her as disgusting, though. Instead, he wished he'd thought to bring some wipes or something to help her clean up. Maybe some deodorant too. As soon as they were left alone for confidentiality's sake, she began to speak in a shockingly articulate voice.

"Please, you have to help me. I have to get back to my kids."

He furrowed his brow. "Where are your kids now?"

"I told them to hide. One is a teenager, and he's watching the baby."

Troy glanced down at his brief. "Says here you're being charged with trespassing."

"It must've been the owner of that check-cashing place. He must've seen us."

"Check-cashing place?"

"Yes, we slept under some bushes across from the store last night. He must've noticed us and reported it."

"Where? On what street?" When she told him, he recognized the location as a bad part of town. Lots of crime and poverty. "You have nowhere else to stay?"

Next came an explanation of her losing her job, which led to her and her children being evicted. They'd lived in her car for a while, but then the car had been towed when they were away. It'd been one long stretch of bad luck, which was something he could commiserate with so much more easily now.

After her came a man who'd stolen nothing but food because he was starving, and several others who, while guilty of their crimes, had acted out of either a sense of hopelessness or desperation. He knew a thing or two about that too. Had it not been for Amber, he would've been in a similar boat.

On the way out that day, he sought the advice of the social services person, focusing mainly on the mother with kids from earlier.

"Hey, I have a client who's homeless and—" The social services person turned to him looking harried.

"Look, I don't have time to do both my work and yours. If you need a list of resources for your clients, just Google 'homeless resources of El Paso' like everybody else." With that, she pivoted on her sensible shoes and strode away.

Troy might not have known what bee had buzzed into her bonnet, but he could follow directions as well as the next guy. He'd managed to keep his smart phone, even though he'd downgraded his service provider, so as soon as he connected to a Wi-Fi signal, he did precisely what the social worker had said. He discovered the locations of homeless shelters—he hadn't even thought about those—food banks, organizations who offered donated clothing, and so forth. Going forward, if his clients needed these services, he'd know where to send them.

At the end of that week, Troy collapsed onto his loveseat feeling bone-tired but more optimistic than he had in a while. It was relatively early in the evening, but he went ahead and prepared for bed, knowing he needed sleep. He'd just lain down when he received a text. Troy squinted one eye at the screen, then smiled.

Sprite: Just checking in with you. Didn't receive any calls about you being MIA, so I'm assuming you showed up to your place of business like a good little boy.

He stared at her text message, torn between a grin and a scowl. A grin because Amber had thought of him, and a scowl because he might've lost his position due to being wrapped up in his own problems. If he'd lost his job, Amber probably would've refused to ever stick her neck out for him ever again. Worse, she'd probably never speak to him either.

Talk about a sobering thought.

Troy: Not planning on going AWOL from this point forward.

Sprite: Good to know. What are you up to at the moment?

Troy: I've already turned in, actually.

Sprite: Hope I didn't wake you.

Troy: You didn't.

The next text he received was a picture. On it was a giant yellow smiley face. It said, "Smile. Tomorrow's going to get worse." He'd shoved out a harsh laugh before being aware of doing so. He'd never thought of Amber as one to go for gallows humor.

Am: Just kidding. I'm sure tomorrow will be better.

Troy: Sure, it will. It's the weekend.

Not that he wanted to mention the previous weekend.

Am: Well, some of us have to be on call this Saturday and Sunday.

Attached to that came a picture of a cat sticking its tongue out. He chuckled at it, then yawned.

Troy: I hope you have a good one, on call or not.

His thumbs paused on his phone's keyboard. He wanted to say more, but he didn't know what. So, he hit send.

Am: You too.

CHAPTER SEVENTEEN

NEARLY THREE MONTHS HAD GONE BY, AND THE CRISP CHILL of winter had given way to another Texas spring. Amber hopped in her SUV, feeling cheerful. After today, she'd have three days off in a row, and she felt so ready for her mini vacay. The hospital had granted her these days at the end of April, which meant the last one would hit on the first of May, an unfortunate coincidence. Also, it wouldn't be three whole days since she had an evening shift to fulfill at the free clinic on the evening she got back, but still.

At this time tomorrow, she'd be at a Corpus Christi beach, sticking her bare feet in the sand. She'd squint out at the aquamarine waves and watch kids play in the surf. She'd hear the seagulls and other ocean birds' caws mixing with the continual crashing rhythm of the tide. All with an umbrella overhead and a romantic paperback in her hand. It would be enjoyable no matter the month. She couldn't wait.

She felt like all her loose ends had been tied up well enough for her to go. She'd met her dad's new lady at dinner a few weeks ago, and after he'd pulled her aside in the kitchen asking her what she thought, Amber had smiled.

"Patti's great, Daddy. You seem very happy together."

"We are. In fact…" Her father pulled a box out of his pocket. Amber gasped.

"Is that what I think it is?"

"Yep," he whispered. "Too soon?"

"You've been dating her for what? Six months?"

"Yeah."

"Then I think it's perfect."

Father and daughter hugged. "Love you, precious."

"Love you too."

To sweeten the pie further, last month a new nurse practitioner had started her training at the hospital, and she was going gangbusters and lightening both her load and Grace's. Troy seemed to be hanging in there too, everything in his public defender position riding smoothly. So with her dad engaged, her bestie surrounded by competence, and her ex no longer crashing and burning every time she turned around, Amber felt like now would be as good a time as any to step away. It wasn't often she could say she had so many of her ducks in a row.

Eight hours later, however, she no longer felt so sanguine.

Troy's last client that day had been a young girl who was barely eighteen. She'd been caught shoplifting, and he'd been able to get her off on a technicality—one thing Amber's ex had always been was an excellent attorney. But when the girl had stood up to leave, she'd collapsed. Amber had been called to the emergency room to consult, and what she'd found wasn't good. Her patient was presenting with all the signs of an ectopic pregnancy.

The girl moaned with pain, clutching her abdomen, and Amber noticed her simple silver wedding band.

"You're married?" The girl nodded. "You're going to need your husband here for moral support when you come out of surgery. Can we call him for you?"

"Um, he's out of reach right now."

"You sure?"

"Yeah. He left about a month ago, but he said he'd be back for me."

Amber bit the inside of her cheek. Apparently, they couldn't count on the husband. She and her nurses pushed the girl's gurney down the hall towards the OR. As she went by, she caught a glimpse of Troy pacing back and forth near the waiting area. Seeing him there acting like a mother hen felt so crazy to her. Prior to his emotional breakdown, her ex wouldn't have batted an eye over someone else's suffering. Yet, there he was, showing up for someone who was a virtual stranger.

Amber felt a sensation of warmth bolt through her. Using terms like compassion and empathy when ascribed to Troy Sykes had once amounted to an oxymoron, but now, that wasn't the case. Her ex had undergone such a dramatic change over the past several weeks that the man's behavior was nigh on unrecognizable.

It was nice to witness.

She pushed the girl through the double doors of the operating room.

"What's your name?" Amber asked her.

"Camille," she panted out, her skin sweaty and pale.

"Okay, Camille. We're going to take care of you now. See you in a bit."

The anesthesiologist put the patient under, and Amber began her work. But the surgery did not go to plan. One seldom seen complication arose after the next, and no matter how many fires Amber put out, another one took its place. She couldn't find all the sources of the bleeding, even though she worked frantically to do so. In the end, her patient's vitals dropped off completely, and the heart monitor made that unbroken sound that meant only one thing.

The girl was gone.

After instructing her most trusted nurse to see if she could track down Camille's husband, Amber trudged out to go back to her offices, only to find Troy waiting for word on his client. Somehow, in all the commotion, she'd forgotten that he was there.

"How's she do—" he trailed off when he saw Amber's face. She reached out a hand to him and tugged Troy to her office.

"She didn't make it," Amber told him as soon as he shut the door.

This wasn't the first time she'd had to divulge bad news, nor would it be her last, but death was never an easy subject for anyone. Too late she registered that she probably shouldn't have told Troy. He wasn't connected to Camille in any deep way and certainly wasn't her next of kin, so technically, he shouldn't have been told before others. At least not if Camille actually had any others. But Troy wouldn't tell. He couldn't under attorney-client privilege. Also, Amber simply trusted that he wouldn't get her into any trouble.

Troy said nothing for a minute, then cursed under his breath. His features warped and twisted into a pained mask, and she wondered just how upset he'd become. Was the man about to break down again right there in her office? The thought made her own eyes burn. Losing a patient, even one she barely knew, hurt. And it'd always been doubly hard on Amber because such situations never failed to make her think of her mother. If Troy lost it, she knew she'd be right behind him.

She stretched up on her tippy toes to touch his broad shoulder. "I'm sorry." The words had hardly left her when he stiffened. He opened his mouth only to clamp it shut again. She pulled back rather than make contact. She couldn't tell what was in his head. "Troy?"

But he didn't respond, didn't look her in the eye. Instead, he hurtled toward her door. Opening it, he paused on the threshold. "Not your fault. Gotta go." Then, he vanished as if he'd never been there to begin with.

Amber went home that night feeling as if she'd been on one of those amusement park rides that did one long free fall. All her buoyancy from earlier had disappeared, erased by the day's events. Still, she had an early flight in the morning, so she went through the motions of getting ready for bed. She climbed in later, staring up at her ceiling. When her alarm went off a few scant hours later, she hadn't slept a wink.

Later, after a layover in Houston, Amber stumbled out of the plane and went to pick up her rental car. Through the large windows of the airport, she noticed the gray clouds, but decided to ignore them. Once she had her rental, she slipped in behind the steering wheel as the first drops of rain splatted against her windshield. She peeked up to see those gray clouds darkening further as they billowed and churned above her.

So much for lying on the beach.

The weather app on her phone said that this storm had blown up from a mild disturbance over the gulf to a full-fledged severe thunderstorm. The rain came down in a deluge that might even cause flooding, and Amber looked out her balcony at the steel mass of whipping breakers and felt glum. Figures this would happen on the first getaway she'd taken in years.

She went out to lunch, getting drenched, then returned to her room looking like a drowned rat. That evening, she decided to order in so she could stay dry. She used one of those delivery services to pick up some Vietnamese food from a highly recommended new hotspot, but by the time it arrived, it not only smelled like cigarettes, it was ice cold. What had the driver done? Left it under an air conditioning vent?

Still attempting to get some modicum of enjoyment out of this trip, she filled her jacuzzi with steamy hot water and took a dip. Remembering her novel only after getting in, she decided she could forego reading for right now. She leaned her head back and closed her eyes, trying to relax. She nearly succeeded, her body feeling loose and warm, when a loud thump came from the next room over. What were they doing over there? Pounding the wall with a baseball bat?

Then, the thumps were joined by the shriek of a saw and hammering noises. Seriously?

Aggravated, she coiled a towel around her middle and stomped over to her phone.

"Front desk."

"Yes, someone is doing some sort of heavy construction work in the room next to mine. Can you have them delay it while I'm here?"

"Oh, sorry, ma'am, but this is emergency work that can't be delayed."

"What do you mean by emergency work?" she asked, puzzled. Had there been a plumbing issue? And if so, why was she hearing hammers and saws? Was the problem with the construction of the walls themselves? Was it even safe for her to stay there?

"A patron reported something we had to see to immediately, but I won't bother you with the details." The young man's voice squeaked, and his words flowed out in a rush.

"We apologize for any inconvenience." Then, he hung up on her.

She glared at the handset, wondering how on earth this place had received a four-and-a-half-star rating. The pings, thuds, and sawing next door went on for another hour, then finally stopped. Amber's bath water had long since gone cool, so she scrambled out, bundling up in some fresh towels. At least they were soft and fluffy. She ordered a pizza directly from one of the nearby Italian joints for dinner and delighted in how hot it arrived.

The aroma floated up like a tangy tomato heaven, and she breathed it in. There were other scents too. The savory meats. The rich vegetables. And it tasted as delicious as it smelled. She'd downed half of a piece when she thought of how many times she and Troy had shared pizza. The last time hadn't been so great, but early on, one of the cornerstone moments of their relationship had happened over pepperoni and sausage. They'd been eating at a quaint café in El Paso, and right before she'd picked up her first piece, he'd rubbed a finger along her chin.

"I'm going to kiss you now, Am," he'd told her, and he had.

She'd dropped her slice, forgetting all about it.

Amber could still remember how soft his lips had felt on her own. How close he'd been to her. How her breathing had stuttered in nervousness as he'd closed in and gusted out again after their contact had been broken. It'd been a memorable first kiss between them, something she'd treasured. And this was the first time in years that she remembered what it'd been like without it renewing her heartache.

As if she'd summoned him with her thoughts, Troy's name materialized on her text app.

Troy: I know you went out of town for a few days and hope your flight was uneventful.

It was a good thing he didn't ask how anything else had gone.

Amber: It did. Thanks.

Troy: Sorry about running out on you earlier. I didn't think she'd die.

Amber's breath caught in her chest. He didn't have to name who "she" was.

Amber: I tried to save her, but not everyone can be saved.

Why they were having such a heavy conversation over texts, she had no idea. At least if she broke down over it, he wouldn't know.

Troy: I know. I've just never watched someone go from fine to a stomachache to dying before.

She didn't know what to say to that. No loss would ever be easy, but sudden losses like Camille's also held a shock factor.

Troy: I've been thinking of how much she looked like Mia.

Oh, no. Maybe Amber shouldn't worry about herself breaking down as much as him. He'd been through a lot in a remarkably short period. And now she felt guilty for leaving to come here because she couldn't be there for him.

She sat up, wanting to kick herself. They *weren't* a couple. While a certain degree of closeness had been building between them lately, she didn't know how to refer to it. Most of what they had in common was a messy past. After everything he'd done, she knew she shouldn't feel such a high level of concern for him.

Yet she did.

She'd watched him become a whole new person over the last few months, a good person. A compassionate person capable of honest-to-goodness empathy. A person she could definitely develop feelings for. Not the old, flawed feelings where everything had been off balance between them either. But new feelings. Healthy feelings. Stronger, longer-lasting feelings.

Snow cones! What was she doing? And where in the world was her head?

Troy: I know she wasn't my sister. I've kept my distance from her and Mom for months now, and I hate it. I miss them both so much.

Amber had typed in **Why don't you call** when she received another message before she could press send.

Troy: I miss you too, Am. As my girlfriend, I mean. We see each other quite a bit, but it's not the same. I wish I could fix things between us. I wish you'd come back to me. I wish I could undo all that I've done because I've ruined things, and now it's too late. Which is sad because I care about you.

Amber didn't know how to respond to Troy's words. Their relationship had been such a roller coaster and putting herself through those twists and turns all over again would be downright foolish of her. That was what her head said anyway. She'd already been down that particular highway. She'd seen how it ended.

Right?

But her heart felt differently. Troy had been so open and candid with her right now. And he'd been acting like a close, personal friend ever since that episode in his apartment. Sometimes, Amber thought he'd had less of a breakdown and more of a breakthrough. He'd become a much better person. And these messages he was sending her? She couldn't have stopped reading them if her room had been on fire.

Which was probably an event she shouldn't picture since it was a few minutes to midnight, which meant it was almost May. Better not tempt fate.

Also, she definitely cared about him. She couldn't seem to help it. She noticed the little ellipsis appear on her screen that informed her he was typing again. It took a while, indicating that either the message would be long, or he was hesitating before sending it. Then, it came.

Troy: In fact, I'm in love with you.

Amber stared at his declaration. He'd never said those three little words to her before, even while they were going out. Which cinched it. There was no way she'd be getting any sleep now.

CHAPTER EIGHTEEN

IT'D BEEN AN HOUR SINCE HE'D SENT AMBER HIS LAST TEXT, but she hadn't responded. He didn't know if she ever would. He'd been typing and everything he'd been thinking about had come pouring out of him, but now, that felt like a mistake. She wouldn't want him like that. Not anymore. He should have known better than to hit her with something like this out of the blue and expect her to squeal and fall into his open arms.

Well, figuratively, since there were currently ten hours of travel separating them.

And he used to think of himself as so smart.

Since he didn't want to bug Amber on her vacation anymore, he did something he'd been afraid to do. He bit the bullet and dialed his sister.

"Troy!" she yelled in his ear, but he didn't mind because she sounded so thrilled to hear from him. "*Finally*. I have so many bones to pick with you."

He chuckled in relief. "Hey, munchkin. Listen, I've been in a bit of a pickle if you want to know the truth, and I'd like to catch you up on everything."

"You'd better."

He did, though he left out the part about Brett shutting him out. And that he'd shut Brett out too. The disconnection appeared to be mutual, and she must know her husband's side of things already. He didn't want to cause trouble in their marriage, and he had no way of knowing the specifics of what his best bud—or *former* best bud—had told her. But the one part that Mia became stuck on was the part he hadn't expected.

"Please tell me you did *not* confess your love to a woman for the first time over a soulless and detached text message. Particularly not to a woman who you've known and dated off and on for years."

"Uh…" This couldn't be good.

"You know, it's a wonder our species manages to go on when the male members of it are this clueless."

"So, you're telling me I messed up."

He heard her make a sound he categorized as somewhere between a scoff and a scream. She hadn't done that since she was little, so this didn't bode well.

"Okay, okay. I can be calm. I can." He heard her blow out a burst of breath, then another one. "Troy, I love you, you know that. But you, big brother, have so much work to do with Amber. And once that's squared away, we'll need to talk about Brett."

"What about him?" He didn't know what was going on with the guy. Had his reputation taken a hit by being associated with Troy's debacle?

"Well, he's convinced that you hate him and won't speak with him."

"But he hasn't contacted me once since all this went down."

Mia sighed. "I suspected as much. But I'm guessing you haven't contacted him either."

"No," he told her, and his tone sounded defensive even to his own ears.

"Well, the good news is that he went into business for himself. It's only Brett Guerrero, Attorney-at-Law, so he's been working primarily out of the house."

"He has clients?"

"A handful. But that number is growing little by little. He didn't want anything to do with those..." She stopped as if trying to come up with the appropriate word. "Well, I won't stoop to calling Bertram and Rockford what they actually are, but suffice it to say that he didn't like what they did to you. One loss does not a failed lawyer make."

Troy swallowed harshly. Since he hadn't heard from Brett, he'd assumed that he must have believed he was as incompetent as the partners had made him out to be. It meant a lot to know that his best friend had sided with him.

"So, why hasn't he called me?"

"Why haven't you called him?" she countered, and he gulped. He'd forgotten how deadly his sister could be with her gibes went she wanted to be. Apparently, arguing effective points wasn't a Troy trait, it was a *Sykes* one. The fact that he hadn't noticed until now just proved how oblivious he used to be.

He'd been batting a thousand across the board with his family. *Not.*

"You two need to go out, do some bro stuff, and talk to each other," she went on. "And by talk, I mean *talk*, really discuss what happened. But my advice is to wait on that. If you're going to have any chance at all with your girlfriend, you're going to have to make *her* your number one priority. You're also going to have to go big or go home since you have so much to make up for. First, though, tell me this. When you say you love this girl, do you mean holy matrimony and forever kind of love her?"

He thought of Amber compared to all the other women he'd ever spent time with. When not with her, his dates had tended to last a single evening. Often only a couple of hours as he promenaded them around at business parties, just to set them loose shortly thereafter with an unfelt, "You're the best."

He despised himself for pulling some of that nonsense with Amber as well. Yet, he'd come back to her. At the time, he'd told himself that it was because she was such a cute, fun girl, but that wasn't true. It was more than that. He'd been drawn to her over anyone else. For years, she'd never been far from his thoughts. And it wasn't because she was a giver or because she'd put up with him the longest. It wasn't even because she'd been there when no one else had.

It was because there was a link between them that felt real and authentic. Being with her felt like diamond rings, and wedding vows, and two point five kids. He wanted her. He wanted her not just now but from now on.

"Yes," he said, feeling one hundred percent sure.

His sister clapped and giggled. "Then this is what you do…"

BEFORE SHE'D LEFT, Amber had told him what time her return flight was due in, so he started bright and early that morning, giving himself plenty of time. Fortunately for him, her best friend, Grace, was cool with being in on it. He'd gone to see her at the hospital and explained what he intended to do, and she'd been onboard. She even had some input on his color choices.

He was about three quarters of the way finished with his display along the outside of the clinic when he saw something that made his stomach both feel light and wonderful and sink at the same time.

Amber was early.

"What's all this?" she asked, moseying up the sidewalk that led to the front entrance.

Troy didn't want to say. At least not till he'd completed everything. But like everything he'd tried to do concerning Amber, even his best efforts seemed too little too late. Despite this, he didn't want to admit defeat.

He'd been in the process of throwing down the gauntlet, for Pete's sake, following his words with visible action.

Twisting the zip ties around the bundle he'd been working on, he stood and approached. Cupping both his hands around her eyes so she couldn't see, he turned her in the opposite direction. "I know it's already ruined, that you've already gotten a glimpse of it, but I need you to not look until I tell you, Am."

"But why?" she asked, squirming as she resisted his hold on her. He stood in such a way that he blocked her view. Since he was basically twice her size, that part wasn't too difficult.

"I'd hoped to surprise you, but apparently, that's not going to work out like I wanted. So what I'm asking—what I'm begging you to do—is to stay facing away until I'm done. Please? Please do this for me?" He felt somewhat devious to plead with her like this, but he was out on a limb here.

She stopped fighting him. "How long is this going to take?" Her words weren't disdainful, though, merely curious.

"Just a few more minutes. Maybe even, like, two. Can you wait?"

Amber blew out a long breath. "I suppose I can. You're being quite enigmatic, you know."

"I know, Am. How about you…" He had to think of something to occupy her. "Tell me about your vacation."

As she started to regale him with her less than ideal experience in Corpus Christi, he released her and bustled around, tying the rest of his display to the building.

"Okay. You can look," he told her, feeling like the entire thing would be anticlimactic, but needing see it through anyway.

There, equally spaced across the façade of the free clinic, were four bundles of helium balloons. Each handful offered a different message. From left to right, they said, "Thank you," "You're beautiful," "You rock," and "You're awesome," in various shades of pink.

He held one last one himself. It was a ginormous one, at least three feet across. This final balloon, in a bright scarlet red, had been personalized to say, "I love you, Amber. Please be mine again."

Since he'd knelt before her the last time he'd asked her to come back to him, he didn't repeat this performance, choosing to stand by the entrance instead. Even though this could no longer be the surprise he'd intended, she stared at it as if she hadn't seen most of his declaration a few minutes ago or the text prior to that. She even raised her hands to cover her mouth. Tears brimmed in her eyes, but he couldn't tell if they were tears of elation and excitement or of disappointment and refusal.

Before he could clarify whichever one it was, an old Chevy pickup even more rusted out than Troy's beat-up Ford Taurus screeched into the parking lot behind them. Well, screeched might not have been the best word. He drifted in sideways like some video game about the Grand Prix. As soon as the tires came to a halt, the driver's side door popped open and expelled a man with an intense look on his face.

Without sparing him or Amber so much as a glance, Mr. Intense sprinted over to the passenger's side and extracted an extremely pregnant woman whose expression was the epitome of terror. Troy couldn't tell if she was frightened because of—probably—being in labor or because of her husband's insane driving. Either one could be the culprit.

The expectant couple vanished through the entrance, and Troy honed all his attention back on Amber.

"So, uh…" he stammered out, feeling anxious about her answer. Ordinarily, he didn't experience anxiety, but that—like so much else—had totally changed. "This is me saying, 'I love you,' Am. Now and for always. How do you, um… feel about that?"

She merely looked at him, her features inscrutable. The longer she went without speaking, the more his nerves went into overdrive. A prickly feeling broke out across his chest, back, and forehead, and the palms of his hands went clammy. Despite being outside, he felt like he couldn't inhale enough oxygen. Also, though the temperature hovered around the seventy-two-degree mark, Troy could swear he felt heatwaves emanating off him like a radiator.

Was this what a stroke felt like?

Eventually, Amber crossed the distance between them. Elevating her hands so that they framed his face, she tugged him towards her. He went willingly, and as soon as his lips were in range, she kissed the living daylights out of him. Euphoria pierced its way through every molecule inside him, and without thinking, he belted his arms around her and lifted her into the air, never once breaking their connection.

After he didn't know how long—counting didn't matter much to him then—she slowly and sweetly pulled her lips from his, but only so she could kiss the tip of his nose instead. Troy had experienced a lot of good times in his life, but nothing held a candle to this. Unlike the brief and almost perfunctory kisses he'd shared with her previously, this one encompassed so much more. Because this time he wasn't just goofing around. This time, he meant it.

"So you're okay with me being in love with you?" he asked her.

"Exceptionally okay."

"And do you…" Dang, he couldn't believe he was going to ask her this after everything that had happened between them. "How do *you* feel?"

She grinned at him, the blue and green of her hazel irises becoming even more vibrant as her eyes sparkled. "I feel like I love you too."

"You do?" Had she really just said that?

She touched her lips to his again, a quick peck. "I do. And do you know what you just did?"

"What'd I do?"

"You fixed May."

He did what now? "Huh?"

She laughed. "I'll explain later. Just kiss me again."

"Yes, ma'am."

He did as requested, then swung her in a circle, making her squeal with delight. But right in the midst of this,

Grace stuck her head out the door. "Hey, I hate to interrupt, but I could use some assistance in here."

"Duty calls," Amber said, sounding rueful. He felt exactly the same.

"Yeah."

"Mind if I call you after my shift? It might be late."

"You can call me anytime, Am. Then, we'll make plans to get together tomorrow."

"Can't wait."

She beamed at him, and with a skip in her step, headed toward the entrance. She opened the glass door, then pivoting toward him again at the last moment, waved her fingers before vanishing inside.

CHAPTER NINETEEN

If someone had told Amber eleven months ago that Troy Sykes would be capable of not just telling her he loved her but showing her too, she would've sneered at them. No one knew as much as she did the kind of man he'd been. If she hadn't seen it and held him in her arms herself, she never would've trusted that the sort of evolution Troy had undergone was more than skin deep.

But in this case, it'd been far more. There had been a fundamental shift happening with him for a long while now, and though she'd suspected at first that he would revert back to the old narcissistic version of himself, he hadn't. In fact, he had only grown more thoughtful and considerate.

She almost couldn't believe that the same man who'd told her he loved her so sincerely just now had hurt her less than a year before. Not that she'd forgotten what had happened. Rather, the memories she had of him since that time had helped to weaken the hold they'd once had on her.

It was a beautiful thing.

Still, she'd promised to relieve her best friend, who had taken this extra shift to cover somebody else, so Amber had better get cracking. She waltzed in on cloud nine ready to share her news with her bestie when she glanced up at Grace, who had her back to her. Not only that, her friend's posture seemed different, on edge, and then Amber spotted the reason why.

The couple who'd entered right before her were standing in the hallway that led to the patient alcoves. Since the clinic had limited space, all three of those alcoves were occupied; Amber could see that the moment she stepped in. Yet the husband was clutching not only his pregnant—and currently crying—wife, he was also clutching something else.

A handgun.

Being a Texas girl, Amber had fired her dad's shotgun, but she didn't know much about pistols. All she knew was that the man was pointing the weapon back and forth between her best friend and her as if he'd handled that gun before and understood precisely how to use it. Instinctually, she raised both palms in surrender.

"Can I help you?" she asked, keeping her tone as nonthreatening as possible.

"Shut up," he barked, and his wife began to cry more vocally. "My wife needs a room, and you're giving it to her right now."

"Sir," Grace spoke up as she cast Amber a tense look, her voice quivering yet adamant. "Like I already told you, we have an obligation to *all* our patients. There are no rooms available. As soon as one is—"

"Shut up, shut up, *shut up*!" he yelled, sounding unhinged. He pointed his weapon at the ceiling and fired, making every person in the vicinity scream. "The next shot is going into one of you two if you don't do as I say."

Her bestie ducked, but Amber held her ground. Or maybe she'd become frozen in terror. Amber could hear heavy breathing from the alcoves, a sign that one if not all of them were in the final stages of labor.

"It's okay. I'll move someone. Just let me check to see which can be moved safely," Amber told him, taking a cautious step toward the nearest alcove.

"*No!*" he shouted with wild eyes, while simultaneously firing.

It took a full beat of her heart for Amber to absorb what he'd done, to register that a searing bolt of fire had entered and exited her upper thigh. The recognition of it impacted her like a set of dominos tumbling forward. A bullet. Two widening circles of crimson stained her scrub pants. The agony of it made her slump backward to land hard on the linoleum floor. The thing must've passed all the way through, which should be good, but it hurt worse than anything she'd ever experienced.

"Amber!" Grace called out, but the damage had been done.

Amber blinked up into the countenance of the man who'd harmed her, still struggling to grasp what had transpired.

His wife flew into hysterics. "Why did you do that? *Why*?"

"You need help," he told her, his features twisted in horror and panic. "They weren't going to help."

"They were too," his spouse howled, shaking her head. "Now what are we going to do?"

"I need to assist her," Grace told the couple as she leaned toward Amber, but predictably, the man disagreed.

"No, you need to assist Carr—" he cut himself off, which probably meant he realized how much trouble he'd put himself in. "My wife."

"Dr. Crawford's losing a lot of blood," her best friend argued, which Amber couldn't believe. Now was hardly the time for a debate. She was doing her best to apply pressure to both her wounds as she took stock of her vitals. Unfortunately, Grace was right. She felt woozy almost to the point of fainting, and there was no possible way she'd be able to stand anytime soon.

This was so not good.

Amber reclined all the way down, attempting to breathe steadily. To distract herself from her peril, she focused on various objects within her sightline. The brightly colored brochures in the waiting area. A black scuff on the creamy wall. The underside of the admittance desk.

It occurred to her then that there was a panic button installed on the staff side of that desk. Not only there but on the inside of each alcove as well. If Grace or someone else could activate one of those buttons, someone far better suited to deal with a gunman would come. Amber could do it too, if she could manage to drag herself over there.

Which was doubtful.

Amber bit back a groan. She witnessed pain day in and day out, but this was something else. It took everything she had not to shriek at the top of her lungs. She'd extend tons more sympathy to her laboring mothers from now on.

Taking as deep a breath as she could, Amber addressed Grace. "Dr. Pendergrass, why don't you take the patient out of one since it's the closest. Remember, everything you might need is under the sink in there."

Her bestie nodded, her too-wide gaze acknowledging Amber's message. The panic button in that alcove was inside the cabinet beneath the sink. And she had to hand it to their patient in alcove one. As Grace escorted her out, she gave one brief glance to the guy who'd caused this mess, then leaned on Grace as she continued her Lamaze breathing. Once the laboring woman had been situated on the floor next to Amber, Grace waved the couple in with her.

Amber could only pray that she'd taken the time to hit the button while the wielder of the weapon wasn't observing her.

Once her patient's contraction had passed, Amber asked her, "What's your name?"

"Marjorie."

"I'm Amber. How far along are you?"

"When Dr. Pendergrass last checked, I was at an eight."

"Okay, that means we should have some more time." Amber seriously hoped so.

"Amber?"

"Yeah?"

"You're white as a sheet." She figured as much. Black spots were encroaching along the edges of her vision. She knew this meant she would soon lose consciousness, but there wasn't much she could do about it. All her worry about Grace and the other patients began to slip away along with her awareness. "Amber? Shouldn't you try to stay awake? Amber?"

The last thing she registered was that someone was tugging on her arm, then, she registered nothing at all.

CHAPTER TWENTY

TROY HAD JUST CROSSED THE THRESHOLD OF HIS APARTMENT when he heard the police scanner go off from next door. He blocked it out, not interested in hearing about another burglary or car accident. He was in too good a mood. But then, he heard something that made him go absolutely motionless right where he stood.

"Squad 111 to 2027 Santa Fe Street," a woman said, probably a dispatcher. That was the address of Amber's clinic. "Receiving silent alarm and a report of shots fired."

"Copy," a man said back. "Is EMS en route?"

"EMS and Rescue are coming, 111."

"Copy."

Keys still in hand, Troy leaped back into his Taurus and slammed it into reverse. Roaring out of the parking lot without regard for its age or general state of wear, he jetted through town, calling Amber's cell and the clinic's line on repeat. Her phone kept ringing then going to voicemail while the main line only gave the annoying *beep, beep, beep* of a busy signal. That in and of itself was unusual, so he stomped even harder on his accelerator.

When he hit traffic moments later, he cursed a blue streak, laying on his horn in frustration. A guy stuck his bearded head out his window. "Hey, knock it off."

"This is an emergency," Troy shouted back, but the other driver just ignored him. Edging up onto the sidewalk, Troy slipped down an alley and came up to another intersection, only to be held up again, but at least he was moving.

By the time he arrived downtown, the entire block near the clinic had been lit up into a red and white flashing nightmare. On the edges, the blinding blue strobes of the police joined the ranks, and yellow caution tape had been strewn around the circumference of the property. Troy parked in the middle of the road and made his way toward the tape, determined to not stop until he knew Amber was okay.

Because she had to be okay. That was the only outcome he could accept.

"Sir, this is a restricted area," a male officer in navy blue said, backed up by a female partner.

"But I have to get to the clinic," Troy told them.

"No, sir," the partner said, shaking her head. "You don't."

"The woman I love is in there," Troy went on, still moving forward, and the two cops closed in on his position. "She's one of the doctors."

"Don't care if she's the pope. You're not going in there," was the male cop's dispassionate response. "Not one more step or we'll be forced to place you under arrest."

That brought him up short. He couldn't help Amber or even check on her from that awful jail cell.

"Can you at least tell me what happened? Is anyone hurt? I need to inquire about Dr. Amber Crawford."

"We have no information we can divulge to the public at this time," the female officer said in that irritating official monotone.

He saw movement out of his peripheral vision and squinted at a stretcher being removed from the building. It was facing the wrong way so he couldn't see who might be on it. As he watched, two more stretchers came out and he could hear the sounds of more than one woman grunting in pain. Was one of them Amber? He couldn't tell, and just like that, his patience snapped like a rubber band.

"Amber!" he called out. "Amber, are you all right?"

For a moment, no one replied, and the pair of officers glowered at him.

"Calm down, sir," the male cop addressed him again.

"Calm down?" he demanded, incredulously. "You won't tell me anything or let me find out about my loved one, and you want me to calm down?" Troy turned back toward the commotion, putting his hands around his mouth in the hopes that someone near the epicenter would respond to him. "*Amber!*"

The stretchers were on the move, and as EMTs swiveled the first one around, Troy caught sight of some blonde-streaked curly hair.

"Officers," a voice Troy could barely hear wafted over to him. "I don't think he'll quit unless you let him inside the perimeter. My boyfriend is super obstinate."

That'd been her voice. Amber's. So at the very least, she was alive.

With a sigh, the two officers who'd been holding him back relented and he aimed himself toward her like a ninety-mile-an-hour fastball.

"Am, where are you injured? What happened? Please, tell me you're okay," he blurted out in a rush, not even coherent.

As he clasped her hand, he noticed that she looked paler than normal and that her hand felt icy in his. Only then did he glimpse up to spot the couple he'd noticed going into the clinic earlier. The man was being situated in the back of a squad car in handcuffs while his wife was wheeled out of the building on yet another stretcher. Troy had seen four stretchers so far.

"I'm going to be okay, Troy. They staunched the bleeding while we were inside, and the IV is helping." She indicated the bag of fluid attached to her arm.

"But what—"

"Shhhh," she said gently, raising a hand as if to touch his face. He lowered his head so she could reach. "I've been shot through the thigh, and I passed out for a minute there. But everything's under control now, I promise."

"Shot? Passed out? I…" Generally, Troy spoke like the attorney he'd been trained as, but now, his words and thoughts were all in a jumble. She tugged on him again, and he touched his lips to her sweat-dampened forehead.

"Shhhh, babe. I'll be fine," she told him again, then quirked her lips up into the semblance of a smile. It was that that made him babble his next words. He was so tightly strung, they sounded like a non sequitur.

"You called me your boyfriend."

Amber released a single soft giggle, her lips lifting higher. It was a real smile, despite everything. "I like you all befuddled like this. You're pretty adorable."

"You're the one who's adorable."

"Are you two always going to be this sappy?" asked Grace, who'd appeared at the doorway of the clinic as she locked it up. Two cops flanked her. She looked as if a slight breeze would knock her over, yet she'd still given some respectable banter. He might've offered her his fist to pound under different circumstances.

"That's the plan," he said. He meant it. Troy had once taken Amber for granted and had to learn the hard way never to do that again. Her calling him her boyfriend meant everything to him. It meant not only that she loved him, but that she'd forgiven him, which had been a privilege he'd thought she wouldn't extend again. Yet, she had.

While the EMTs were focused on the other women—all of whom appeared to be in different stages of labor—Troy seized his opportunity. Cushioning the back of her head with one of his palms, he leaned over her and pressed his lips to hers. She seemed so fragile right then that he did this as gently as possible, but she had other plans. Surprising him, she sat up a little and deepened their connection, making the careful peck a real kiss.

It was a kiss Troy felt flowing through him like water from a baptism.

"Dr. Crawford, we need to get going," one of the EMTs said, and Troy took a half-step back.

"You heading to Le Mesa?"

"Yes, sir."

He kissed her forehead again before severing their contact. "I'll be right behind you."

EPILOGUE

Two Years Later

"You're doing good, Am. Perfect, even," Troy murmured to Amber as she breathed more heavily than she ever had before. Being an OB/GYN meant she was already an expert at Lamaze breathing, but teaching it and doing it were two different things.

"Yeah, well, I kind of want to smack you right now, so whatever," she said, not meaning those words, but incapable of snatching them back either. She'd anticipated handling the process better than this, but the pain was killing her. She'd never thought anything would be as terrible as her bullet wounds, but she was pretty sure she had a contender.

Her dad and stepmom had stopped in before things had intensified, which she was so glad of in retrospect. Brett, Mia, and Brett's mom were out there in the waiting room with them, probably pacing. The only people she felt okay about seeing her like this were her staff, Grace, and her husband. It'd been dramatic enough when her dad had barreled into her hospital room after she'd been shot a couple of years ago and found Troy looped around her like a boa constrictor. Her man hadn't wanted to let her go.

Not much had changed.

Even if having her husband at her side wasn't doing much to diminish her pain, she'd never want him to be anywhere else. Having Troy's undivided attention and support meant everything to her. Still, she needed to move this process along. She glanced at the clock again. It was 11:30 p.m. on April 30th, and the notion of being in hard labor during the month of May seemed imprudent, even if she knew it was a silly superstition.

Yes, Troy had declared his love to her on May 1st. And yes, she'd told him that he'd fixed the month for her. But having their first child during the same month that had brought her so much distress throughout her life made her antsy.

She and Troy had been married for a year and a half, and they'd tried to schedule this pregnancy better. Yet, fate had other plans.

Her admittedly irrational feelings about May evaporated as her contraction clenched down so severely she nearly screamed. Then, the inevitable came, and she felt the same compulsion women had been feeling since the beginning of humanity.

"Gotta push, Grace," she grunted out a heads-up.

"All righty, then," her bestie said, snapping on a pair of gloves. "Let's make this reservation for Sykes, party of three."

Amber pushed, putting all her effort into the correct muscle groups. At least some of her knowledge and experienced helped. As she caught her breath, she caught a glimpse of her husband, who was aiding her in the process of sitting up.

"You've got this, Am," he said, swiping a kiss to her sweaty temple. Then, when she went to push again, he braced her back as she'd instructed him to do. The pain increased, and she pushed through it again.

Several exhausting minutes later, Grace announced some good news.

"There's the head. We're almost there."

With another series of pushes, Amber delivered her baby with a loud cry. The gurgling shriek of a newborn pierced the room next, and a moment later she heard her best friend's revelation over her own huffing and puffing.

"It's a girl."

That was how all the ultrasounds had looked, but it was lovely to have final confirmation. Amber blinked over at the clock to see that the minute hand had just coasted over the numeral twelve. Their daughter's birthday would be May 1st after all. As she studied her ten flawless fingers and ten tiny toes, Amber decided she could live with that.

A few moments later, their beautiful baby started nursing for the first time. Troy rubbed his thumb through the downy hair along her teensy little temple.

"Am," he whispered, "I can't believe she's finally here."

Amber took in the transfixed expression on her husband's face. Already he was in love with their baby. They both were.

"She has her daddy's blond hair," Grace mentioned. "Are you ready to disclose this child's top-secret name?"

Amber almost laughed. "Call everyone else in here."

She and Troy had kept the name they'd chosen under wraps for months. Once everyone else had ranged themselves around the room, cooing, oohing, and aahing, she glanced at her husband. It was time for the big reveal.

"Everyone, meet Keiko Rose," Amber and Troy said in unison, proudly.

"For your mom…" her dad croaked out, his voice sounding like gravel. "She… she would've adored that."

"Wow, Am," Troy whispered, his tone just as rough, so she peered up at him. His bright blue eyes were streaming, but he didn't seem to mind. Neither did she since hers were doing the same. "You're amazing. Look what you've done."

"What *we've* done," she corrected him.

"Well, I'll be contributing a lot more from here on out, but this part was ninety-nine percent you."

"Good input, man," Brett said from his place along the wall. "Happy wife, happy life." And Mia proceeded to bop him on the arm. Troy's sister was six months along herself with their second, and his mom carried her first grandchild, Stevie, as he slept in her arms.

Amber felt thrilled to be one of the first mothers to deliver in her and Grace's new private practice clinic. It'd taken a lot of effort, but now their fantasy had become a reality. Even better, they qualified for a grant that allowed their less fortunate patients to receive most, if not all, of their care for free.

Brett's cell rang, and he hurried out to answer it, indicating that it must be a client. After Troy had mended fences with his best bro, the two of them had worked for nearly a year to open their own firm together. Her husband had left behind his days as a public defender but continued helping those who most needed it by offering his services on a pro bono basis. Maybe due to this, his reputation as the #LawyerNeedsALawyer had faded into obscurity. He was now one of the most highly rated defense attorneys in the southwest.

Not that life would always be perfect. Their marriage was a partnership that was ever evolving, and she knew that troubles would come and go. But as Amber brushed her lips across first her husband's cheek, then their daughter's, she knew everything they'd been through had been worth it and then some.

I HOPE you enjoyed reading *A Rude Awakening for the Ambitious Ex-Boyfriend*. Writing about bad boys for a clean and wholesome series has been fun and enlightening. Of course these characters aren't perfect by any means. They have flaws. They have faults. They're not all necessarily nice. But I've always believed that every person is redeemable if they want to be. I'm thrilled to have found enough redeemable men to match them up with their perfect matches in this series.

If you've missed any of the stories in the series, find them all here:

Texas Redemption Complete Series

THE SILVERSTONE RANCH is the setting for the next cowboy series. Take a look at Book 1!

Marguerite won't trust any man again, let alone a method actor. Cade's determined to convince her of his sincerity. Then circumstances force him to break the one promise he made her—and she may never be able to forgive him.

When everything is an act, how can love be real?

The Movie Star Becomes a Cowboy

WANT ANOTHER FREE SWEET ROMANCE?

If you enjoyed this sweet billionaire romance, I'd love to give you another one for free! Join my readers group and you'll receive a copy of *The Billionaire's First Love* as my gift to you.

Jack's back home after eight years away. Tracie isn't prepared to see him again. When she does, she realizes he still has her heart. They'd started out as best friends and even then she loved him. Can they pick up where they left off? Is life that simple? Is love ever that easy?

Tap here to get your copy of The Billionaire's First Love

ABOUT APRIL MURDOCK

April Murdock loves romance, especially sweet stories that make you sigh out loud. She loves to write stories inspired by people in her life – past and present. Okay, so truthfully, she's never known a billionaire or anyone from royal bloodlines, but taking reality and pumping it up a bit is what makes it fun!

April has lived her whole life in the Southern US. Traveling is a great love, but coming home to Georgia where her heart is makes her happy. April is married to her high school sweetheart. Their children are married and they can't wait to have grandchildren to spoil.

∾

Connect With April on Facebook

April's Website

Made in the USA
Middletown, DE
18 September 2022

10712527R00109